Also by Alice Mead

Dawn and Dusk

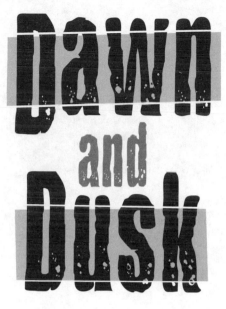

ALICE MEAD

Farrar, Straus and Giroux • New York

The author gratefully acknowledges Dr. Steven L. Burg, Adlai E. Stevenson Professor
of International Politics, Brandeis University, for his critical reading of the
manuscript.

Distributed in Canada by Douglas & McIntyre Ltd.
Printed in the United States of America
Designed by Symon Chow
First edition, 2007
10   9   8   7   6   5   4   3   2   1

J Mead
Main

www.fsgkidsbooks.com

Library of Congress Cataloging-in-Publication Data
Mead, Alice.
    Dawn and dusk / Alice Mead.— 1st ed.
        p.   cm.
    Summary: As thirteen-year-old Azad tries desperately to cling to the life he has
known, the political situation in Iran during the war with Iraq finally forces his
family to flee their home and seek safety elsewhere.
    ISBN-13: 978-0-374-31708-9
    ISBN-10: 0-374-31708-9
    1. Iran-Iraq War, 1980–1988—Juvenile fiction.   [1. Iran-Iraq War, 1980–
1988—Fiction.   2. Family life—Iran—Fiction.   3. Iran—History—
1979–1997—Fiction.]   I. Title.

PZ7.M47887 Daw 2007
[Fic]—dc22

                                                                    2006040850

For Ziya, Jeff, and Mike

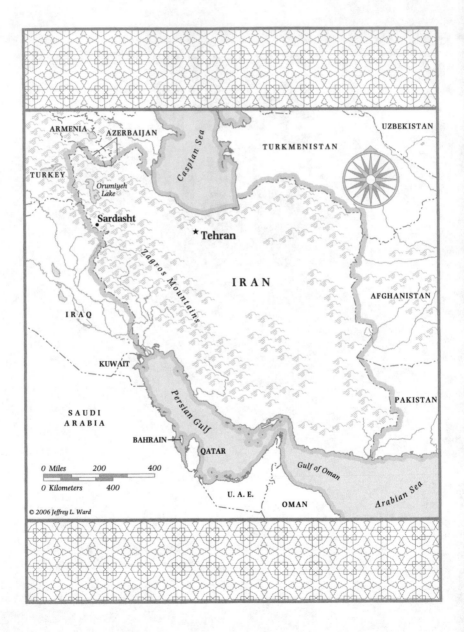

Introduction

With the advent of a global economy, the traditional view of America's role in the world as the defender of freedom for all fails to take into account the realities of profit-making, dwindling resources, and international trade, which also define our interests. Nowhere do our competing visions—of bringing freedom to those who live under dictatorships and of protecting resources—clash more dangerously than in the Middle East, especially in the area that holds more than 50 percent of the world's oil reserves: Saudi Arabia, Iran, Iraq, Kuwait, and the United Arab Emirates.

Located between Africa, Asia, and Europe, the Middle East is a geographic region currently comprising about twenty countries. Each is a complex mix of ethnic groups, languages, religions, and cultures. The Middle East is also the birthplace of the world's great monotheistic, prophet-based religions: Judaism, Christianity, and Islam.

The modern Islamic Republic of Iran is a large country to the east of Iraq made up of thirty provinces. It was the center of a vast ancient empire, called Persia by the ancient Greeks. Today the main ethnic groups in Iran include Persians, Azeris, Arabs, and Kurds, with nearly one million Afghani refugees and approximately 95,000 Iraqi refugees. The official language is Farsi (Persian).

Since the 1950s, the United States, the United Kingdom, and other countries have been trying to gain political influence over Iran's oil and gas reserves. In 1980, the Islamic Republic of Iran was in the throes of violent political and religious upheaval. The Shah (a king backed by the United States) had been overthrown the previous year by a Shiite religious leader, the Ayatollah Khomeini. Harsh religious laws were being enacted in Iran, and its vast network of secret police was being given a free hand in enforcing them.

Taking advantage of the turmoil, Saddam Hussein, the dictatorial leader of Iraq, seized southern oil-rich regions from its much larger neighbor. That was how the eight-year-long Iran-Iraq War began, and how weapons of mass destruction started to collect on both sides of the borders as various allies joined in. Russia and China sold weapons to Iran, and the West sold weapons to Iraq, including chemical weapons.

In the seventh year of the war, "Saddam Hussein directed

his war machine against the Kurds"[1] on both sides of the Iran-Iraq border. Previously he had kicked the Iraqi Kurds off the oil fields of Kirkuk, driven them away from the Iranian border, destroyed nearly six thousand villages, and killed thousands of their inhabitants. Saddam's chemical attacks against Sardasht, Iran, and later against Halabja, Iraq, were part of a detailed plan of genocide called Al-Anfal. A Kurdish leader said at the time, "There will be no more Kurds left in Kurdistan. Saddam's plan is to destroy us as a people."[2]

The Iranian Kurds live among the beautiful Zagros Mountains in western Iran. The Kurds are the region's fourth largest ethnic group. Kurdish culture is one of the world's oldest, dating back to the times of Abraham, Noah, and before. Kurdistan is what these 20 million people call their homeland. It is a territory that includes regions in Turkey, Iraq, Iran, and Syria, but in each country Kurds have been marginalized and subjected to forceful repression. In 1987, in Sardasht, this repression reached a terrible climax when Iraq's Saddam Hussein used chemical weapons as part of his plan to get rid of the Kurds for good.

"Weapons of mass destruction," a term we have heard often since the 9/11 World Trade Center and Pentagon attacks

---

1. Jonathan C. Randal, *After Such Knowledge, What Forgiveness?: My Encounters with Kurdistan* (New York: Farrar, Straus and Giroux, 1997), p. 210.
2. Ibid.

in the United States, were actually used against the citizens of Sardasht, Iran, in an incident that has since been called "the Third Hiroshima." Few people are aware of the story of how the Kurds survived the chemical bombings in their town. It is our story as well, and we need to know what happened.

Prologue

We are sitting in our cramped apartment in America, in the state of Maine. It is early evening and snowing out. Maine is a cold place. My mother is peeling an orange for us, and we are drinking tea from the fancy tea glasses my Aunt Avin smuggled out of Iran. It makes me smile to see them here. Not one of them broke on our trip through the mountains. She wrapped them in her socks.

The orange sits on a plate now, divided into sections, pieces of an orange sun that once was whole. I think maybe I am like that piece of orange, set adrift. It seems I will look anywhere for traces of who I am and where I came from, for mirrors of myself.

I lie back against the pillows. The taste of the orange bursts in my mouth, and I crawl into my dream place while the adults talk—about jobs and English class and the grocery store. My dream place is a gazebo with delicate arches covered in ornate, flowery blue-and-white tiles. I smell red roses. I dream bumblebees. I am in the shade, but the hot June sun surrounds me.

And in the dream I am very young. I am caught up! Up! My father swoops me into the air. My mother is snapping a photograph and laughing. They are happy.

I *know* they were happy. They were! But then everything changed.

"**A**zad! Wake up!"

I ignored my father's voice and rolled over, drifting back into the warmth of doughy-sweet sleep. Ah. A little more rest would be so delightful.

"Get up!" my father, Omar, yelled again from the living room.

Oh. School! Was I already late? I sat up with a start, sweaty in the tangled sheets. Glancing at the clock—it was barely 6:00 a.m.—I jumped out of bed and grabbed my shirt.

Yesterday my best friend, Hiwa, and I had been two seconds late for homeroom. Two seconds! Okay, maybe thirty seconds. And Mr. Azizi, our Persian teacher, had hit my hands with his ruler. But Hiwa, who not only was late but had messy hair, he beat with a rubber hose on the backs of his calves. Mr. Azizi told us both to get our hair cut.

"Hey, Bibi!" I took the cloth drape off my parrot's cage. She looked at me sideways, tipping her head down affectionately. I put a handful of seeds in her cup and made sure her water dish was full. Usually I took her out for a few minutes and talked to her. I told her stories from school, my secrets, my wishes, how Hiwa had a crush on Avin, the beautiful woman my uncle was going to marry in less than two weeks.

"Sorry, Bibi. I can't play now. Be a good girl while I'm gone. Okay?"

I hurried into the bathroom and splashed cold water on my face, glancing at myself in the mirror. I tucked my shirt in, then ran my hand over my short black hair—or what was left of it. Yesterday Hiwa and I had stopped after school at the barbershop and gotten our hair cut as short as possible. I turned my face from side to side to see if any sideburns had grown in overnight. Some guys in my class even had faint mustaches. At thirteen. But not me.

Oof! That barber had scalped us. Oh, well. Better looking like a shorn sheep than getting hit with the rubber hose.

I went into the living room. My dad was sitting on the sofa, where he slept, still in his T-shirt and boxers, smoking a cigarette, staring at the floor. Probably he'd come in late again. He looked tired and hungover, not the least bit ready for his job laying bricks all day.

"Hi," I muttered as I went into the kitchen. He didn't answer. Another bad mood, I thought in disgust.

I checked our kitchen for food. There was a small piece of a chocolate bar in the door of the refrigerator. I ate that quickly. But I was starving! I was tall and skinny and could eat like a horse without getting the least bit fat.

"What happened to your hair?" my dad asked from the doorway.

"I got it cut short for school. How come there's never any food?" I asked. Now I would have to go to the bakery next door.

After my mom had left, he didn't even try to run the household. Buying bread and fruit and cheese on a regular basis seemed to be beyond him. He had let the roses in the courtyard grow into a tangled mass of half-dead branches, which he finally cut down to the roots. I'd loved those roses, but he didn't care.

"I'm no cook." He shrugged. "And don't go racing off to your mother's for food. You go there much too often. Find something else to do once in a while. You should hang out with the kids in the neighborhood more."

I stared at him. What was this? I loved visiting my mother and uncle. My father had never said I couldn't go there before. Why had he brought this up? But I didn't have time to argue, or I'd be late. I grabbed my book bag from the chair.

"I have to go." I crossed the living room and headed out the front door. He always made it sound as if my mother had betrayed us, had betrayed me. Even though she was sweet and kind and loving, she'd had to leave me behind. That was how divorce was in Iran. Children over seven had to stay with their fathers. I never understood exactly why my parents had divorced. And I couldn't get an answer from my father or mother. When I asked my mom, she just smiled and changed the subject. I wished there was some way I could find out.

"See you later," I said.

"By the way, you're not going to your Uncle Mohammad's wedding either. And I don't want you hanging around his crazy friends anymore. You hear me?" he called as I ran down the steps.

Not go to the wedding? There was no way my father was going to stop me. Anyway, over the next two weeks, he'd forget what he'd said.

I hurried across our small courtyard to the bakery next door.

"Good morning!" I called through the open door. The sun was just starting to stream in the front window of the shop, and the two clay ovens were already hot in back. I set my book bag on a café table. Wusta Fatah, the baker, peeked out to see who was there.

"Hey! Good morning, Azad!"

"Azad! Azad! Ooooh!" called his wife, Hero, hurrying from the back and squeezing my face. She handed me two fresh rolls in waxed paper, one filled with chocolate and one with cheese. She slipped me a sealed cup of liquid yogurt to drink.

"Thank you!" I grinned. They were always so good to me.

"No breakfast again? Is your dad home?" Wusta Fatah asked.

"Yeah. But he came in late."

His wife gave the baker a warning look.

"I hope Omar slept soundly. There was a roundup last night because of people like him. SAVAMA took in twenty young men off the streets."

I looked down, blushing. SAVAMA was Iran's dreaded secret police.

"Fatah! Azad is a fine boy. Just like his uncle," the baker's wife said sharply. "He has nothing to do with the police. He's a child still. Don't worry him with things like that."

"A child? Ha! It's time he grew up," the baker said.

Now my father's sullen mood this morning made more sense. It had nothing to do with me and everything to do with what had happened last night. Maybe he simply wanted me to stay closer to home because he felt panicky about the latest roundup. I knew that my father was an informer for the secret police, but it was something no one ever dared to bring up openly, something I tried not to think about. Even though Wusta Fatah seemed to believe my dad had been involved in the roundup, I didn't.

Wusta Fatah looked at me and shook his head. "Okay, okay. Never mind. Tell Omar that if it weren't for us, you would starve!" Then he retreated to the hot ovens in the back, grumbling.

I bit into my chocolate roll. The crumbly bread melted deliciously in my mouth.

"I wish you were living with your mother, you know that? She's such a wonderful woman," Hero said.

I shoved the rest of the pastry into my mouth. The news about the roundup was bothering me. Was I being too trusting? Could my dad be involved in things like that? Why was he suddenly telling me where I could go? Whom I could see? He was getting so weird!

I knew I shouldn't talk with anyone outside the family about my parents, but at that moment I felt I could trust Hero. She always had a good word for my mom. Of all the people I knew, she would be honest with me.

"Hero, why did my mother and father get divorced?" I asked in a low voice, not wanting Wusta Fatah to hear. "Please tell me."

She didn't answer. She acted as if I hadn't spoken.

"Here. Sit down to chew your food. You don't want to choke." Hero sat down at the café table with me and changed the subject. "Oof. I'm tired already. You know how early we have to get up. I didn't sleep well last night. Did you hear those planes overhead, Azad? Very low. But no bombs."

"It wasn't a bombing run!" Wusta Fatah called from the

back. "It was an Iraqi reconnaissance mission, that's why! They were spying on us!"

"Oh, nonsense. Why would they fly a spy mission at night? It's dark out. Do you think they're owls?"

"Women! You don't know anything! The Americans gave Saddam night vision equipment. Trust me. The Iraqis can see us sleeping in our beds!" Wusta Fatah was nearly shouting. "First the Americans spend years financing the secret police for the Shah, and then they give our mortal enemy planes worse than anything imaginable. What are they doing to us, those crazy people?"

"I'd better get going. Yesterday Hiwa and I were late."

"Oh ho! Really?" The baker laughed.

I grinned. "Yeah. The teacher beat us. But it wasn't my fault. It was Hiwa. You know how lazy he is. He gets up as late as possible."

"He could stand to lose a little weight," the baker said. "Or he'll look like me soon!" He patted his own round belly.

"Bye!" I called. Outside, I finished the other roll quickly and brushed the crumbs off my shirt. Then I ran down the hill, skidding on loose pebbles that had washed down the hillside in the rain. Stopping at the corner, I peeled the foil cover off the yogurt and drank it, enjoying its cool, smooth, tangy taste. Yogurt was so much better than the boiled milk my father brought home in used soda bottles.

I was in the boys' middle school, where I studied the Persian language; Arabic; math; science; tech education; and electronics. And history. Persian history, not Kurdish history. We weren't allowed to speak Kurdish in school.

I slowed down, thinking about what Wusta Fatah had told me. Had my father been involved in the arrest of those young Kurdish men last night? I only knew that he hadn't come home until late. That didn't mean he had anything to do with the roundup.

Innocent or not, the men would be tortured and executed. They would join the thousands of people who had "disappeared" from our city of Sardasht during this war because the Ayatollah was afraid of a Kurdish revolution. My father might be lazy. He might drink when he shouldn't. But he would never be part of such a terrible thing! I was sure of it.

• • •

It was 6:30 a.m. when I got to Hiwa's gate. He had promised to be on time today and waiting for me outside. I couldn't believe he wasn't there. Impatiently I threw a pebble at his window.

Tap! Another one. Tap!

Where was he? We had a secret call we used to get each other's attention. The bray of a donkey, only backwards. Not *eee-aww*, but *aww-eee*. Anything to do with donkeys was pretty funny. The word *jash*, "donkey," was the name for an informer.

I cupped my hands. *"Aw-eee! Aw-eee!"*

There he was at the window, waving. Why hadn't he come out to wait? He must have been trying to eat as much as he could before I arrived.

"Come on!" I shouted. I was so annoyed: first my dad saying I couldn't go to the wedding, then Wusta Fatah telling me my dad was involved in the arrests, and now Hiwa making us late for school again.

He came out through the metal gate in the garden wall, calmly chewing on a large hunk of fresh-baked flatbread his mother had made.

"Here. For your lunch." He handed me a roll filled with rice and spiced meat. I stuffed it in my bag.

"Thanks." When I told my dad that people gave me food each day, he'd said, "The kindness of strangers is a blessing." For him, it certainly was. For me, too.

"We have soccer today in phys. ed. Can't wait," Hiwa said.

Hiwa loved soccer, but since he didn't like running up and down the field, he played goalie. He liked diving to the ground to make spectacular saves. He didn't notice the bruises he got. Hiwa was like a camel; he never felt pain. He hadn't even cried out when Mr. Azizi beat him with the hose yesterday. All the guys had been impressed and had crowded around us at recess. Hiwa bragged that it had simply felt like being hit with wet spaghetti.

We came to a section of streets where the sidewalks were

crammed with metal kiosks. Street vendors were just set-
ting up shop for the day, unloading boxes of shoelaces, apri-
cots, chocolate, batteries, cheap pants, toys, and scarves for
women. We inched by them.

"Listen, after school, first let's walk by the girls' school and
then go to that electronics shop. The new one near the city
center? Maybe the owner will let us play with that Atari he
has. I want to play the Pac-Man game."

There was only one shop in all Sardasht that sold the electronics games we were obsessed with. But I wanted to tell
Hiwa something.

"Yeah. Pac-Man. Cool. Hiwa, listen. I think the baker's
wife knows the real reason my mom left. I'm going to find
out."

"The real reason? What do you mean, 'real reason'? She
left because your dad's a grouch. What other reason could
there be?" Hiwa looked at me, puzzled.

"None," I said. "Forget it. Hey, there's a soccer rerun on TV
this afternoon. You want to watch that instead of going to the
shop? It's Pakistan versus Australia."

"No way. We have more pressing concerns."

He pushed his way through the crowded sidewalk and I
followed, thinking about the silly Pac-Man game, the blue
screen with the funny circle-headed guy chomping his way
along the pathways of the maze while the silly music played in
the background.

"Americans play really fun games," I said. "Maybe they're not such bad people underneath."

"Of course they're bad," Hiwa said. "They're greedy. They never give to others. And their women are barely covered. What kind of people dress like that in public? They have no modesty at all!"

"Yeah." We had Morality Police who roamed the streets, making sure women were properly veiled and not wearing lipstick or flashy jewelry underneath their robes.

"They're worse than bad. They're evil. Be careful or they'll give you the evil eye! Waaaah!" Hiwa leered at me. I pushed him away. We began to scuffle. He was such an idiot.

There was a Revolutionary Guard patrol vehicle with four guys in it, one of their Toyota Land Cruisers, parked right across the street. The men were buying cigarettes at a kiosk.

"Cut it out! Quit pushing!" I said. "You want those guys to come over here?"

"Like I care." Hiwa laughed. "Come on. I'll race you to school."

I ran after him. As always, I felt a little jealous of Hiwa. I wanted his fate, his family. I didn't want mine.

We tore along the dust-choked streets, past bakeries, hardware stores, kiosks, grocers with boxes of fruit on display; past taxis, vans, and mule-drawn carts from the surrounding villages. We darted past another Guard patrol, holding our book bags so that they would be clearly visible. I hoped we wouldn't be stopped and asked for our I.D.'s. That would make us late for sure.

We ran through the school gates and clattered up the stairs to the second floor. Our class was at the end of the long hall. Thirty-five boys stayed in that room all day, while the teachers of each subject came and left, hour by hour.

We edged our way past the rows of battered wooden desks and took our seats near the back only a moment before Mr. Azizi came in. I glared at Hiwa. "That was too close. Wake up earlier tomorrow," I whispered.

He smiled. "Why? We made it, didn't we?"

Mr. Azizi began to take attendance in his deliberate way. I

got out my book and glanced at my notes on Persian mythology. Yesterday's lesson had introduced the great mythical bird the Simorgh. A gigantic eagle-like bird, part lion, part dog, with huge wings, she lived in the Tree of Knowledge and knew the secrets of fate. One wing was fortune, the other grace. Kurds had stories about her, too.

"We were starting that poem about the thirty birds who traveled to the land of the magic Simorgh, right?" I asked Hiwa. I thumbed through my notebook, looking for where I'd left off. The teacher was purposely ending the year by introducing us to his favorite poem. I had gotten a copy of it from Uncle Mohammad.

Hiwa nodded. "I wonder if the Gray Flamingo was on that journey. It was only eight hundred years ago," he said mischievously, barely holding in a laugh. "Did any flamingos go on that trip?"

"Ssh!" I whispered, elbowing him. Our nickname for Mr. Azizi was the Gray Flamingo because of his stiff gray hair and jutting face.

He glared at us from under his bushy eyebrows. We were quiet while he finished with attendance. Then we had to rise and say a pledge to Iran and listen to a prayer reading, after which we sat down, waiting for the lesson to start.

I had my pen out and notebook open, ready to take notes on the first lines of Attar's famous poem. I'd read sections of it the night before, lying in bed. Hiwa clearly was not interested in what we were doing. He lived for tech. ed. class and spent his time designing circuitry patterns in his notebook. Right now he was writing the word *motherboard* in Arabic script. I tried not to laugh.

The Flamingo got up and stood staring down at his desk, his lips pressed tightly together. He made no effort to start the lesson. We all glanced sideways at one another, wondering what was going on. Weren't we going to do the bird poem? I liked the story—the long journey, the hardships and vices that defeated bird after bird: the greedy partridge, the arrogant hawk, the duck who didn't want to leave his stream. It had to be something political, or why would the teacher act so nervous?

At that moment, *boooom!* The air outside shattered. Hiwa and I jumped. War planes from Iraq flew overhead, just above the treetops, on their way back to Iraq from a bombing run on Tehran. *Boooom!* Again! I winced in fear. A bomb? I looked out the window for smoke, braced myself for the shuddering of the earth. No. The planes had just broken the sound barrier. It happened all the time. They flew faster than Mach 1 to terrify us. The noise was deafening and the glass in the windows rattled. Then they were gone. Outside, the birds went crazy with fright.

We waited. Above the blackboard was a large portrait of

the Ayatollah Khomeini, our religious and government leader, our absolute ruler for life. Iran used to have a shah, but there was a revolution when I was younger. Then, while the country was in turmoil, Iraq seized some of Iran's territory in the south. And ever since, there was this endless war with Saddam Hussein. Hundreds of thousands of men and boys had been killed, buried in special cemeteries, martyrs for Iran. Hundreds of people from Sardasht had died in bombings by Iraqi planes, and the city center was in ruins. Why did they bomb our dusty little town? We had only one park, one cinema. Was it simply because we were Kurds?

Looking at his watch, the Flamingo finally spoke. "Today we have a change in schedule. A captain from the Revolutionary Guard is coming to talk to us. He's a high-ranking official to whom you must show absolute respect. He has come to speak with us about civil preparedness. Resistance is an important part of any war. And because we are so near the border with Iraq here, your preparedness is of the utmost importance. He is going to talk with you about—" The teacher stopped. He pressed the back of his hand to his mouth.

The Gray Flamingo, crying? We were stunned. I looked at Hiwa. What was coming? A military-style lecture full of death-to-America stuff? Or was it something new about the war? Maybe the war was over and we had lost! Would we be forced to become Iraqis?

There was a brisk rap at the door. Mr. Azizi turned abruptly as a military officer in a gray jacket and dark blue pants entered and shook the teacher's hand. The entire class stood, arms stiff at our sides.

"I am Captain Bahri Farzin of Iran's Islamic Revolutionary Guard Corps. You may sit," he said. "Boys, I want you to remember every word I say today. Children play a role in war. One of our holy martyrs, a boy of thirteen, a young man just like you, has only this week sacrificed his life beneath the treads of Saddam's tanks. That young man is already in heaven."

A photo of this kid had been on the news day after day. None of us made a sound. Was the captain here to make us join the Army? I was suddenly terrified. Most Kurds ran away if they were forced to enlist. No one wanted to fight for a regime like the Ayatollah's that considered us second-class citizens.

Captain Farzin clasped his hands behind his back and paced back and forth in front of the room.

"First I'll tell you about an ancient wise man: Solon, the giver of laws. He lived more than two thousand years ago, during the time of King Croesus, who was the richest king in the history of the world. Croesus had mountains of gold, heaps of gold. And yet he wasn't entirely happy. Those who think they must have everything are never happy. So the King sent for the wisest man of that time, Solon, and asked, 'Solon, who is the happiest of men?' And Solon said, 'Fate is unpredictable. No man can be deemed happy until the manner of his death is known.' "

Hiwa and I looked at each other nervously. The manner of his death. Whose death?

"Boys, that young man gave his life for Iran, dying bravely in the line of fire. His was a good death, a glorious death. We are at war against a terrible enemy. The Iraqi regime led by the madman Saddam Hussein will do anything to win this bloody war. We have collected evidence through our infiltrators that he may plan an illegal attack against Iran. And he will do it and get away with it because the world doesn't like us. Iraq has powerful allies, like the United States, who want us defeated. You can be sure that if atrocities are committed, the world will be silent if Iranians are the victims."

My thoughts whirled. We weren't victims. And we were children, not young men! Iranians loved their children passionately. Even my mixed-up father loved me in his own way. I knew that as surely as I knew the sun shone in the sky.

The captain wrote three letters on the blackboard. *Sh-M-R.* "Now"—he tapped the board—"this is what you must be prepared for."

Beside the letter *Sh* he wrote "chemical weapons." Beside the *M* he wrote "microbial weapons," and beside the *R* he wrote "radioactive weapons."

"We think that Iraq has these chemical weapons and that

they were given to them by the British, the Swiss, the Dutch, the Americans. This is not a secret. It's a fact! Saddam has already used chemical bombs against our Army's rear guard with varying rates of success. But we didn't think even the devil Saddam would use them against an unarmed city. And, indeed, he may not. But you need to be prepared.

"Let me tell you about this. A chemical bomb doesn't cause a fire or make a blast hole in the ground when it's dropped. No. It explodes high in the air—poof! And a cloud of poison gas rains down on everyone and everything below. When you breathe in this poison, it will burn your lungs. It will burn your eyes and skin. So what can you do if this should happen? Stay indoors. You can soak towels in water at home and cover your face. Wear long, heavy clothing to protect yourself. If you're trapped outside, go to high ground because the gas is heavy and will sink into low valleys. Understood?"

No. I didn't understand a thing. I couldn't think properly. Was he lying to us? Our government often said crazy things, which we kids simply ignored.

The smartest boy in our class, Sirwan, had raised his hand. "Can we be given gas masks for protection?"

Praise God for Sirwan, I thought thankfully. There was an answer to this horror.

"Gas masks would work. Of course," Captain Farzan said. "But right now we're still equipping our Army with them. As soon as we have extras, they'll be distributed to all of you. You will be taught how to use them."

A sigh of relief ran through the room. Gas masks. Those would save us.

Sirwan raised his hand again. "Please, sir. Are you going to move us to a safer city for now? One not so close to the border?"

Now the captain looked annoyed.

"Of course not. Move thousands of people? There are twelve thousand people in Sardasht. Be realistic. I've told you how to be prepared. If you cover your mouth, nose, and skin, and you have towels to wash with afterward, you will be safe."

We wouldn't be relocated. We wouldn't have gas masks. We were looking at one another, puzzled, desperate. Many boys had their hands raised now. A lot of kids were calling out questions. Wasn't there something called nerve gas? Would it paralyze someone for life?

"All right, all right. That's it for today," the captain called out. "Remember: when you pray, bless the martyrs who fight for us."

The captain shook our teacher's hand and left quickly.

"Mr. Azizi! Mr. Azizi!" the boys were calling out.

"Silence!" The Flamingo clapped his hands for order. "I have nothing further to add. There is nothing I can tell you. Please. Speak to your parents about this. For now, it's important to remain calm. Remember that this is only a remote possibility. Calm down, boys. Please."

"Calm down? And how is that possible?" whispered Hiwa. "The Flamingo's gone nuts."

I knew Hiwa was trying to joke to make me feel better, but I couldn't smile. How could he keep his sense of humor at a time like this? I thought I was going to throw up.

"Books open! We will read a few passages from *The Conference of the Birds*. This is a wonderful tale, this journey to an unknown future, an unknown land. These thirty birds, the falcon, owl, finch, peacock, and so on, are willing to travel beyond the veiled and impassable mountains, seeking the magic land of the Simorgh. As you know, the author is the Sufi poet Farid ud-Din Attar, who lived in the twelfth century, and his overall theme is the unimaginable brilliance of the love of God."

Mr. Azizi began reading about the soft throat of the dove, the sparkling blue of peacock feathers, the little stories of lost love, torrents of ancient history. The soothing, flowery language filled the room like a sweet-smelling balm, blocking out the horrors Captain Farzin had told us about.

As the teacher read, I tried to concentrate on images— lush red roses tumbling along our courtyard wall, the springtime meadow full of wildflowers near my grandmother's village. For a while I was successful. But then my thoughts began bouncing around madly. The rose, ancient symbol of love, bloomed sweetly but lasted only a day. Gold was simply a metal that we foolishly adored. The world was transient. We could lose it all in a moment. That was what Attar was saying. And he was right!

The inside of my head felt hollow. Occasionally I got migraines, and now I saw images of butterfly wings flashing in a sunny spring meadow, first bright, then in shadow, yellow, then gray, and rubbed my eyes. Light and shadow. The play of light fluttered and danced just behind my eyes.

• • •

All day, through class after class, teachers came and went as if nothing had happened, as if the captain had never come. Later, out on the sunny playing field in phys. ed., I felt the flip-flopping wings of light as the dizzy feeling came back.

But it couldn't! Right now I had to play soccer. We, the yellow team, had the ball. We were dominating the pale blue team 2–0.

I was a striker. I was supposed to be chasing the soccer ball, but I felt vulnerable being outside and exposed. What if the planes came now? I thought of what Wusta Fatah had said, about the reconnaissance planes they'd heard last night. Could the Iraqis see us in our beds? Would they poison us while we were sleeping or playing soccer? I would run away.

Not just because I was tired of living with my father, but because of the war. Maybe I could get Hiwa to go with me.

Three-quarters of the way down the field, I stopped running and bent over, my hands on my knees. My teammates were hollering at me to move. I walked in a circle, shaking my head. I wanted something, but I didn't know what. I supposed I simply wanted that lecture not to have happened. I desperately wanted to return to the day before and began to daydream that I had.

"Hey! Azad! Move it! Get back in the game!" *Tweet!* The phys. ed. teacher shouted and whistled, starting toward me to whack me in the back of the head. Reluctantly I began running. It was either that or get beaten.

e didn't go to the electronics store after school. I backed out.

"I can't, Hiwa," I said. "It's too hot and I have a headache. Maybe Sunday." We walked up the dusty street from school, past the shops to his house. Behind us a taxi was trying to drive on the sidewalk to get around two parked vans that blocked the street. The taxi driver honked at us to move over.

"You shouldn't drive on the sidewalk!" I yelled. "Idiot."

"It's just a dumb taxi," Hiwa said, surprised at my anger. "Relax, Azad. Don't worry so much. Who knows why that guy came to talk with us today."

"It's not just that. It's my dad."

"Why? What did he do? Did he beat you because we were late to school yesterday? My dad said he was going to, but he never got around to it."

"No. No. Nothing like that. Well, he said I can't go to Mohammad's wedding. But that's not it, either. I can't explain. Listen, Hiwa. Did you ever think of running away?"

He stared at me. "Not really. You mean you might? Where would you go? Do you have family in Germany or something?"

"No. Never mind."

"Well, here's the important thing to remember: school's nearly out! One more day! How great is that?"

"Yeah. Summer." I smiled. "See ya."

I started home, thinking about summer vacation. I usually spent it with my mother in her village in the nearby mountains, playing day after day with my cousins Hossein and Leyla. Maybe Hiwa was right about the captain. Maybe nothing terrible would happen. The captain just wanted to scare us. I'd try to put it out of my mind. But I'd ask Uncle Mohammad about it as soon as I got the chance.

• • •

Our house had three rooms. You entered a small courtyard with apple trees, a walnut tree, the hacked-up rose bushes, and a small pool covered with leaves on the bottom. Up a few steps and into the living room, the kitchen, and my bedroom. Feeling somewhat less woozy, I went to my room and fed Bibi cracked sunflower seeds and talked to her for a while, lying down with my eyes half-closed. I told her about the Iranian Army guy and what he'd said.

"Mr. Azizi told us not to worry, Bibi. And if the planes do come, I'll save you. I'll cover your cage with a wet towel. You'll be okay."

Bibi grabbed the cage door with her beak and tugged it, trying to get me to let her out. I opened the door and she climbed onto my finger. After I lifted her out, she sidled up my arm and perched on my shoulder, nibbling the edge of my ear.

"You're getting to be an old lady, you know that?" I took her into the bathroom and let her look in the mirror. She turned her head from side to side, looking at her reflection.

"I'll read you the bird poem later, okay? But you have to go back in your cage now."

I stretched out on my bed.

Dawn and dusk. That's how we Kurds thought of our lives. As soon as we had hope and thought a new day was dawning, bringing the possibility of something good, something to hold on to, we lost it—sometimes through our own fault but sometimes from things others did to us.

I felt like a coin tossed in the air, spinning. My father on one side, my mother on the other, each claiming to be the good one. Good on one side, bad on the other, and me, the coin, flipping and falling, tumbling over and over, now good, now bad, now light, now dark. I barely knew which was which.

I didn't want a two-sided coin. I wanted a coin with only one side: the bright, sunny side when we all lived together.

That was the coin I used to have but seemed to have lost for-ever.

I remembered my early childhood as heaven, as Hiwa's still was. Maybe kids everywhere remember their childhood this way—sunny, safe, smelling of beautiful red roses. I re-membered playing in the pool of water in our courtyard. I re-membered kisses, cousins, celebrations that lasted for weeks. And then it all stopped.

When I was seven, my father, Omar, was taken away by the secret police. He'd been caught drinking alcohol, which was against the law, but the police didn't need much of a rea-son to arrest someone. They would simply torture him, inter-rogate him, and see what use he could be to them. Three days later, my father came home covered in bruises, with enough money to buy a small TV set.

After he bought the TV, he and my mother began fighting bitterly. I hid outside in the garden, listening to their angry voices, my hands over my ears, and wished that they would stop, that the sun would come out every day, that the roses would smell as sweet as before. But that wasn't what hap-pened.

One morning when my father was out, my mother came to me, dressed in her long gray coat, a black scarf tied tightly over her cloud of dark, wavy hair. My uncle stood behind her with her bags.

"I'm leaving, Azad. I'm divorcing your father," she whispered. "I can't stay with him any longer, and one day I'll explain why. I'll visit you as often as I can. He has agreed to the divorce and won't oppose our seeing each other."

"No!" I screamed and threw my arms around her. "I'm going with you! You can't go!"

"I have to leave. I can't live with this kind of compromise. Sooner or later, you'll be caught up in it. I can't let that happen."

I heard her words, but I didn't understand her at all. What was she saying? Our lives were happy. They were glorious.

She pulled my arms loose and put them at my sides. I ran at Uncle Mohammad and tried to kick him in the shins to make him leave. Maybe this was his idea somehow. Tears streamed down my mother's face. She picked up a cage from the floor that, in my distress, I hadn't noticed. In it was a large green parrot. She handed it to me.

A bird? What good was that? I didn't want a parrot! I wanted my mother!

"This is Bibi. Isn't she beautiful? And so gentle. Take good care of her. Do it for me, Azad. Remember, I'll be at Mohammad's. I won't be far away. I'll talk with you as soon as your father allows it."

And then they left. I was standing at the table, alone. I ran into the street, but the car was already gone. She'll come back, I thought. Nothing in the world could make her leave me behind. So I sat right down in the middle of the street to wait.

After a while a van full of villagers on their way to the mountains crawled up the hill behind me and honked.

"Hey, kid! Get out of the way! Come on. We have a long drive!"

"Who cares?" I yelled at them.

I climbed up on the roof and stayed there for hours. My father had to come get me in the evening. He tried to talk with me a little, and said he was sorry that things hadn't worked out with my mother.

"Will she come back tomorrow?" I asked.

"Sure. She will. If she has time," he said.

But she must have been busy. She didn't come. Three days went by.

Every day I asked, "Will she come back today?"

"I don't know," my dad answered. "Maybe."

I kept this up till finally he said angrily, "Can't you understand this? She's not coming back at all!"

She would come. He was clearly wrong. He was a person without patience, without devotion. I was not.

I moved Bibi's cage to a small table next to my bed and spent hours talking to her, stroking her soft feathers with my finger, waiting for the day when my mother would come for me. Maybe it would be tomorrow. Or the next day. Or the next. And so I became a dreamer. And finally Mom did come. She took me to a pastry shop for a treat, and told me that I could visit her at Uncle Mohammad's whenever I wanted. From then on, I visited her as much as I could. But it wasn't the same. The dark, scared, fluttery hole in my heart was always with me. My shadow.

• • •

My headache subsided, and I settled down on my bed to do what little homework we had for the last day of school. Later, when the sun started to go down, the heat outdoors would let up. Then the kids on the street and I would gather, running around like maniacs, playing soccer and rooftop tag till it got dark.

My math review problems took only minutes. But I couldn't concentrate on my Persian homework. I was supposed to recite a poem about the usual stuff. Love and loss. Full hearts, love lost, and the pain of a lifetime. Bittersweet memories. Fate intervening, keeping people apart when they wanted to be together. Blah blah blah. The words danced on the page. Why keep an open heart at all, then, if it was only going to hurt you? Hiwa was writing a poem about his unrequited love for Avin, my Uncle Mohammad's bride. Didn't people have anything else to write about besides love? I shut the book and sat up. I was determined to press Hero for the truth about my mom.

In the afternoons I sometimes helped the baker and his wife clean up after their long day in exchange for pocket money. I went next door. Hero was there, alone, sweeping flour dust and bits of crumbly dough toward the front of the shop. A ceiling fan spun lazily overhead. Wusta Fatah had gone out in their van to buy more sacks of flour for early to-morrow. I took the broom from Hero and kept sweeping. Without a word, she got an orangeade from the cooler for me to have later. She poured herself a glass of tea, then sat at the café table.

When I finished sweeping, I sat down. "Come on, Hero. Please don't ignore me. Tell me why my parents split up!"

"Why do you want to know?" she said finally. "It will only lead to trouble."

"Because! Suddenly my dad is telling me I can't visit my mom, I can't go to the wedding. He's gone crazy." I glared at her.

She sighed and shook her head. "You're a stubborn one, aren't you? All right. I'll tell you. This happened six years ago, in 1981, after the police first took your father. A very crazy time. Fatah and I had a niece, his sister's daughter, who was nine years old at the time, and since we had no children of our own, we loved this little girl very much. But then Fatah's sister died and her husband lost his job. His factory in Tehran, an automobile factory, closed and he wanted to emigrate. Instead of simply leaving the girl with us, he arranged for her to be married to a fifty-year-old guy, a man with two other wives. We argued with him, but he was determined. It was terrible. So Fatah and I begged your mother to help us. She was so brave and smart, I knew she'd think of something. She and another woman went to the village and helped the girl escape. They changed her I.D., her name, clothes, everything. They created a new life for her."

"And did the girl survive? Do you know where she is?"

Hero didn't answer. "If I knew, I wouldn't tell you. Shall I go on? So. When your father was taken in for interrogation, in order to receive less torture he told the secret service what Behar had done. After that, the Morality Police came to check on your mother. She was arrested several times. You can't imagine how Fatah and I felt, Azad. We had asked her for help."

I was jealous of that little girl! Why on earth had my mother helped her, a child she didn't even know? "She should never have gotten involved with something like that!"

"I'm sorry, Azad. Sometimes life reaches out and pulls us in ways we could never imagine."

"Not Hiwa's family," I said resentfully.

"So far they've been lucky. But who knows what the future holds for them?" Hero said.

"I have to go," I mumbled. I jumped up, knocking the café chair over accidentally.

Hero righted the chair. "Perhaps I shouldn't have told you. You're so upset, Azad."

"No, no. I wanted to know. It's just—she never told me. All this time."

"Because you're still young. That's why! We live in a time when it seems the only way to protect our loved ones is to keep secrets. What if she had told you and it turned you against your father? Then what? As it is, he has tried to care for you as best he can. I'm sorry, Azad."

"No, no. It's okay."

● ● ●

What a crazy day.

I climbed the ladder to the roof and lay down on my back in the one shady spot. I could hear large bumblebees buzzing in the jasmine and the apple tree and could smell the thick-scented roses in the neighboring gardens. A tall mimosa tree spread its leaves above my head like a lacy veil. Through it I could see the clear blue sky. I stared into the blueness, wanting it to reveal my fate so I could be prepared. Tomorrow was such a mystery. For everybody! How could I have imagined the confusion of today? How could I ignore it, like Hiwa?

The sky calmed me. The sharp, clear blueness was steady

and unbroken, extending forever into outer space. Whom did the sky belong to? To Saddam, so that he could use it to fly in and kill us? No one owned the sky. The sky above me should be mine, a shaft rising straight up from my head, free of bombs and planes forever. A peace shaft, full of grace and fortune.

Pale insects fluttered overhead, clear and shiny as cellophane with the sun shining through their nearly transparent bodies. Okay, I would share my sky space with insects and butterflies and birds. And clouds. And stars. And rain. But that was it!

On hot nights my dad and I sometimes slept up here under the stars. There was a tiny star in the Small Bear group. It was so small that not everyone could see it. This was the wishing star in Adam's coffin, my grandmother said. Whenever I saw it, I always wished the same thing: that my parents would be together again. But now that I knew exactly what had happened, that dream was lost forever. How could I stay with my dad, knowing what he'd done? I would run away. Somewhere up Gurda Sur, Red Hill, the steep hill that led to my mother and uncle's, I would make a secret hideout for myself in a ravine overlooking the city. That was my new daydream, but it felt thin and frail as insect wings.

Below me, our gate clanged shut. I glanced over the edge of the roof. It was just before five and my dad was home. He tossed his masonry trowels in the corner of the courtyard and went inside to wash before the next call to prayer. I had expected to be furious when I saw him, but watching him from above, seeing the tired sag of his shoulders, the pale gray mortar dust in his black hair, his heavy steps in the cement-crusted work boots, I was surprised to discover I felt sorry for him, too. How worn down he seemed, how tired.

After the divorce, he hadn't run off and left me. He hadn't dumped me on some distant auntie or left me with a smelly old farmer with no teeth, who would have worked me half to death. I climbed down the ladder and put out some bread and figs and laid his prayer mat out for him.

When he came out of the bathroom, he was surprised. "Thank you, Azad. It was a long day."

"For me, too."

As the call to prayer echoed from the minarets, we knelt down and prayed together. I hoped for peace, at least in my heart. But I couldn't focus on praising Allah at all. Why should I, when my life was such a mess? My frustration came surging back. My father had betrayed my mother. How could I feel sorry for him?

And what about the arrest last night of those twenty men? I had to confirm that he hadn't been involved. Should I ask him about that? Tonight I would confront him, I decided. We'd talk—about everything! Maybe some of the confusion could be cleared up.

But there wasn't time. He ate quickly, put on a clean shirt, and went out without a word. He started his Lada and drove off, leaving me alone. I sat at the table resentfully. Why would he never talk to me? Well, if my dad wouldn't, I knew that my mom and Mohammad would.

I slammed the gate behind me and ran through the wind-
ing back streets up Gurda Sur to my Uncle Mohammad's
house. In ten minutes I reached it and opened the door, slipping my shoes off right away.

"Mom! Hey!" I yelled. "It's me. Azad!"

My mom came running from the kitchen, where I could
see she'd been cutting up fruit and making tea. She seized my
face in her hands and kissed both cheeks repeatedly until I
protested dizzily. "Okay! Okay!"

"How is Bibi?" she asked.

This was like a code with us. It meant, Was I okay? Was
my father treating me well enough?

"Bibi's fine. Is Uncle Mohammad here?"

"Yes. With some friends. I'm going to serve tea in a
minute." She looked at me more closely. "Azad. Are you sure
you're all right? What's wrong?"

I dropped into a chair, overcome with the day's news. I
didn't know what to tell her first.

"Hero told me about how you helped her niece escape that forced marriage!" I burst out. "And how Dad turned you in. I can't believe you kept this a secret from me! You should have told me yourself so I wouldn't have had to ask the neighbors. You don't trust me at all, obviously." My voice choked with bitterness.

My mother knelt in front of me. "Of course I trust you, Azad. But remember, you were seven years old at the time. It was in 1981. Terrible laws were being enacted against women. Nine-year-old girls could be forced to marry."

"Laws? So what? I don't care about laws!" I said, raising my voice. "You left me. You cared about that little girl you didn't even know more than about me. You sacrificed our family for her!"

"No. No, I didn't. Perhaps it seems that way, in the heat of the moment because you're angry now. There is no truth in passion, Azad. Only reflection and the passage of time bring truth. We were divorced because your father gave my name to please his supervisors. He betrayed me."

"Why didn't you tell me?" I sulked.

"Because you had to stay with Omar by law and I didn't want to interfere with your relationship with your father."

"But," I said, "I still don't get it. Why did you decide to help Hero? And who was the woman Hero said went with you to get that little girl?"

She hesitated. "Azad, listen. I am fighting, too. But not with guns." There were tears in her eyes.

Just then Avin, Mohammad's fiancée, came into the room, apparently wondering what had happened to the tea. She saw my red face and my mother's tears and quickly hugged her.

Avin turned to me. "Please, Azad, whatever it is, leave it for now. Mohammad has guests. Abdullah is here."

Oh, yes. Guests. Hospitality first. Family problems would be smoothed over. That was how we were.

"I'm sorry, Mom," I said.

"Yes. Me too." She smiled at me and blew her nose. "Hey! Nice haircut," she said.

"Yeah." I tried to smile back.

I went to the door of the living room, where a group of men—I thought they were old, but they were probably around thirty—all with thick black mustaches, were sitting on the floor cushions, talking politics as usual. Mohammad's crazy friends. None of them was married yet; Mohammad would be the first. They hung around the cafés and went to soccer matches. I liked them. They were interesting and always seemed to know a lot about what was going on. They were talking about the Democratic Party of Iranian Kurdistan, PDKI, the Iranian Kurdish party that was pressing for our equal rights and even for a separate state that they called Kurdistan. I had to wait politely for Mohammad to greet me.

"Come in, Azad. You know everyone, don't you?"

I shook hands with each person, murmuring hello in a soft voice. Then I sat on the floor.

My mother came in with the tray of tea, nuts, and fruit and set it on the low table. She sat down beside me.

Avin served the tea and then sat next to my mother. She was wearing a dark skirt and jacket with a crisp white blouse and a pale green scarf at her neck. She looked very beautiful and very young. Mohammad was thirty, but Avin was only twenty-two and a medical student. Hiwa mentioned her age to me all the time. I felt myself blush. Hiwa's crush made me self-conscious about Avin's beauty. My mother noticed my confusion and smiled.

"I want to tell you something that happened at school today," I said, interrupting the conversation.

Mohammad looked at me sharply. The men stopped talking. We tried to seem so casual, so careless, living life day to day in a normal way: weddings, shopping, school, roof tag, tea. But the truth was, hundreds of thousands of Iranian men had been killed in the past seven years. Everyone was scared. Any change in routine reminded us of that.

"Today a captain in the Revolutionary Guard came to my class and told us about chemical weapons. He said there might be a poison gas attack. Here. In Sardasht!"

"You mean mustard gas?" My mother gasped. "That's it! We should leave. I won't stay in this godforsaken place."

"Behar," my uncle said quietly, "let Azad finish."

My mother's eyes were wide. Beside her, Avin looked frightened, too, but didn't say anything. She folded the edge of her skirt into tight pleats, let it go, and folded it again. I saw that her fingers were shaking.

"Maybe he came just to scare us," I said. "That's what Hiwa said. These bombs explode high in the air, not on the ground, and they make a dust cloud overhead."

My uncle's best friend, Abdullah, who'd lost his right foot in a bombing attack in downtown Sardasht, said, "Aah, perhaps this is a carefully placed rumor. I'll check tomorrow with a friend in the Army and see what he can confirm. Saddam's been gassing Iranian soldiers for three years. The hospitals in Tehran are full of soldiers poisoned by chemicals. They have to stay on oxygen for life . . . if they live."

"It's one thing to attack our soldiers, another to attack civilians," my mother said bitterly. "To gas an entire city? Women? Children? Elderly people? There are international laws to protect women and children from attacks in warfare and from chemical weapons in particular. This threat is a criminal act. An act of genocide!"

I stared at her. She sounded so fierce! All these years she had created a cocoon of gentleness around me, hiding her real self. Now I saw she was a fighter!

The men were silent, everyone locked in his own thoughts.

"This war! Seven years of—of what? Half the time we have

no electricity. The economy is in ruins. And have you heard the religious broadcasts? Khomeini wants to take over Iraq itself, not just get our land back!" Mohammad said. "This kind of chaos is exactly what makes foreigners continue to be involved in our affairs. The Ayatollah came into power saying we would be free of outsiders. All our weapons come from outsiders now. So do Saddam's."

I didn't want them to talk about international politics. I was thinking of Bibi and how to protect her. I looked around at the grownups. I thought they should make a plan. "If it happens, it's best to run to higher ground because the gas is very heavy. So I'll come here, Uncle Mohammad, because you're much higher up Gurda Sur. Oh, and, Mom, save bottles of water."

"I already save bottles of water," my mother said.

"They should evacuate us, of course," Abdullah said. "If we weren't Kurds, they would. They would take us to a safe haven, not leave us here like sitting ducks."

"The captain said they might bring us gas masks," I said.

Abdullah laughed. "Oh, yeah? You think the Guard patrols will bring a present for us? Imagine Americans getting such Christmas presents from their CIA. Oh, Santa. What did you bring me? A lovely gas mask? Why, thank you very much." He pretended to slide it on over his face. "Fits perfectly. Looks so nice on me."

Everyone laughed to relieve the tension.

"*Did* Americans send the chemicals to Saddam?" I asked.

Abdullah shrugged. "Even if they didn't give him the poisons themselves, the Americans are supporting Saddam in his war against Iran. That's for sure. I've seen American officials shaking Saddam's hand on TV. The West hates our Ayatollah. And they want to protect the oil in Kirkuk from us Kurds and keep it for themselves," he said.

"Don't talk to me anymore about oil or Kirkuk, Abdullah!" said my mother. "That's in Iraq, not here. You think that somehow we are now after centuries going to create a Kurdistan, redrawing borders to suit our interests? The dream of Kurdistan is a prison. I don't care about it anymore. We should report this terrible threat to outsiders and begin to think of protecting ourselves."

"Protection?" said Abdullah heatedly. "It's PDKI who will protect you, Behar! That's precisely the point! If these bombs come, they will be targeted at us. We Kurds have to stay organized. Now more than ever!"

At that point it became clear to me that Abdullah was a member of PDKI. Wow! Didn't he care about the danger he was in? I admired his courage, even though it also frightened me. The secret police chased Kurds halfway around the globe to find and kill a PDKI activist. He winked at me as if he could read my thoughts. I ducked my head.

Mohammad reached over and ruffled my short hair.

"How is Hiwa today? The West has so many new technical inventions. Our boy Hiwa knows all about them, right?" Mohammad said in an effort to change the subject.

I smiled.

"You know what, everyone, we need to finalize the wedding plans," my mother said. "After school lets out tomorrow, Azad, I want you to go to Wusta Fatah's and borrow some strings of lights to hang in the courtyard. Can you do that?"

"Sure." Hiwa's family also had some lights, which they often used in the courtyard in the summer. Those would probably be enough. My mother and Avin started talking about how much rice, lentils, honey cakes, walnut cookies, and so on would be needed.

More than one hundred guests were coming. No matter what my father said, I would be there! I wondered if Hiwa and I, being thirteen now, would be placed with the men or with the women and children for the feasts. But I couldn't concentrate for long on the wedding talk. Neither could Avin.

"Mohammad?" Avin asked. "Do you think we should postpone the wedding? With the threat of those bombs and the arrests, maybe it's not a very good time."

"Come on, Avin! We can't let circumstances push us around," Abdullah said. "Right, Mohammad? Go ahead with the wedding, I say. We're looking forward to it!"

Mohammad smiled at his fiancée. "The preparations are practically finished, Avin. Everything will be fine."

She lowered her eyes and said nothing. I could see she was annoyed that Abdullah had interfered and that Mohammad had taken Abdullah's side. She got up to clear away the tea and fruit.

I let the conversation of the adults drift above my head. We lived in two places—Iran and Kurdistan, an imaginary but ancient land; a country defined only in our dreams. For centuries we'd kept this dream alive, living apart from the Arabs, the Persians, and the Turks, staying in the high mountains, using the caves and secret paths and our tribal alliances for protection. But with computers and spy planes and poisonous bombs and the *jash* on all sides to betray us, how would we survive?

I went into the kitchen. Avin was washing the tea things in the sink, a set expression on her face.

"There's no hot water again," she muttered. "The electricity must have been off earlier. And we're completely out of lemons. I can't stand tea without lemon."

"I can go get some."

"No. That's not the problem."

She wasn't usually short-tempered.

"Are you angry with Abdullah?" I asked. I was. I felt like he pushed everyone too far.

"He scares me. He has nothing to lose, Azad. He's not married. He's been in the Army. He'll sacrifice everything for the cause of Kurdistan. I don't want Mohammad and me to live our lives that way, always under some kind of political shadow that we can't escape because of what we believe in. I agree more with your mother. We have to stand up for our rights, but we must take care of ourselves at the same time."

I nodded and picked up a dish towel to help her dry the little glasses.

She continued. "Honestly, Azad, I'm afraid about the wedding now. I'm afraid something will happen to prevent our happiness."

"It won't, Avin. Everything will be fine. And how about your exams? Are you done for the year?"

"No. Two more to go. Tomorrow. Chemistry and anatomy."

"Maybe once they're over, you'll feel better."

"Don't worry. I've got them aced!" She grinned at me confidently.

"I'll finish the dishes," I said.

"You will? Okay, thanks. Then I'll go study."

The last day of school came and went. I stood at my desk and stumbled through the recitation of the love poem I'd memorized. The teacher gave out awards. I got a certificate of recognition in Persian mythology of all things. Hiwa got an award in electronics.

After school I went to Hiwa's house for a big lunch to celebrate. His mother served us kebabs, pilaf, and pudding. I ate till I thought I would burst. I looked down at my belly and patted it. It felt round and solid.

"Looking forward to summer?" his mother asked. "Will you be going to your grandmother's village?"

"Yeah. Hey! Maybe Hiwa can come for a week or something," I said. "Do you want to, Hiwa?"

"I don't think so." Hiwa wrinkled his nose. "Probably not."

It annoyed me that Hiwa didn't love going to the mountains the way I did. He got bored there in five minutes and hated helping with the chores. He never did chores at home.

His mother spoiled him because he was the only boy. That was my opinion.

"I think you should come. You can take the van. It's only two hours."

"Yes, Hiwa," his mother said. "I think you should go for a few days. The mountains are so healthy. The air is fresh. You should get out more, get some exercise. Why not?"

"I'll tell you why not. There's no electricity up there! It's smelly! There are goats running around biting your pockets and pulling on your pants. And Azad has to shovel manure."

"City boy!" I said.

"I'll talk about it with your father," Hiwa's mom said.

"Spare me," groaned Hiwa. "Why did you have to mention this, Azad?"

I grinned.

We pushed our chairs back. We didn't have to help clear the table or do the dishes. Hiwa's two younger sisters would do that.

"Come on upstairs," Hiwa said. "My poem about Avin is finished. I want to see what you think of it."

"Oh, no." I trudged up the narrow stairs behind him.

"Oh, yes."

"The wedding is in twelve days, Hiwa. Give it up. She's lost to you forever." We entered a small bedroom with two pullout divans, where he and his sisters slept. He took the poem from the wardrobe where he kept his winter sweaters, and unfolded the paper.

"Ready?"

"I guess so."

"What stars shine from her dark eyes,
What roses bloom on her soft cheeks.
Her hair flows like the torrential mountain streams,
But my yearning stays trapped in my heart."

"Not bad," I interrupted. "Is that it?"

"No. Now would you shut up? Just listen, okay?

"My face cast down in sorrow,
No music fills my throat.
I've lost my love at nightfall
Before the day could start."

I wanted to say something silly, but found I couldn't. Hiwa's poem had actually moved me.

"That's really good," I said. "So, I mean . . . Do you really feel that sad about the marriage?"

"Yes." He folded the paper carefully and slid it back under the sweaters. "This is my first real love. I always want to remember what it felt like."

"I guess love poems are okay," I said. "But I liked the bird poem. You know, the one we were doing when the captain came? The one about the birds traveling to find the Simorgh?"

"It's so ancient! Classical poetry about Sufi stuff? Come on, Azad."

But I *liked* the stories about the birds, the greedy parrot, the deceitful peacock who let the snake enter the Garden of Eden, the kings and princes and wandering dervishes, the search for light. I had been telling Bibi all of this before I went to sleep. Hiwa would tease me mercilessly if he knew!

"We'll have fun at the wedding. I promise," I said.

He smiled wistfully. "You will, maybe."

"You will, too. Hey. Did you ever tell your parents about the captain and the chemical weapons?" I asked.

"Yeah. They said he was just trying to scare us Kurdish kids. They said not to pay any attention."

I nodded. I bet that was what most parents had told their children. I didn't tell Hiwa the comments Abdullah had made, about foreigners sending weapons or the Ayatollah wanting to take over Iraq. We sat there in silence for a few minutes, Hiwa probably mooning over the loss of Avin, and me fretting about the meaning of fate and whether I would ever find true love.

"Oof," I said finally. "I think I ate too much. I better go home."

• • •

In front of my house, three younger boys were aimlessly kicking a purple plastic ball. Clearly, they had been waiting for ages for me to arrive. When they saw me coming, they begged me to play with them so they'd have a fourth.

"Oh, all right," I grumbled. My stomach felt less over-stuffed after my walk. "But I don't want to play soccer. Let's go up on the roof and play tag."

My father had gotten home early for a change. The front door was open and I could see inside. He was smoking and sitting at the table, staring at our tiny TV. Yesterday's soccer match on the sports hour, probably. Pakistan versus Australia? But I didn't want to go inside right away. He might nag me about the wedding.

The other kids and I climbed the ladder to our roof. On one side there was a narrow alley and Fatah's bakery, but on the other the neighbor's house was very close to ours and it was an easy leap from rooftop to rooftop. First, though, we had to choose who would be it, a decision that took at least five minutes of loud arguing.

Usually, as an older kid, I would be a major contender in the argument. But I was still in such an odd mood that I didn't join in. Before the captain came, everything in my life —school, my mother, Bibi, even the yogurt I drank every morning—had been fused together like a glass globe. Only I didn't know it until now, when it wasn't that way anymore.

Now my life wasn't a globe. It had been shattered by dread. It was like pieces of broken glass lying in the dirt. I was staring down at the bits, not knowing how to pick them up and put them back together. I took the ball and bounced it off my head. I felt like kicking it high into the shadowy sky and drifting clouds, watching it disappear.

The kids argued on and on. They were taking forever. Who cared who was it? I decided I wasn't going to leap from roof to roof like a demented mountain goat. Let them do that. I climbed down the ladder.

"Hey! Come back, Azad," one of the kids yelled down at me. "Where are you going? Don't you want to play?"

"No!" I shouted back. "You argue too much. You're a bunch of babies." I went inside.

"Well, well, if it isn't Azad," my dad said. He was pouring tea for himself. "School go okay?"

"Yeah. It was the last day." How could he not know that? I didn't mention my award. He didn't tell me what he was doing, so it seemed only fair.

"Oh. Oh, that's right. Yeah. I forgot. There's some goat cheese here, if you're hungry. Help yourself."

"Okay. Thanks."

He pushed a plate of cheese and bread toward me. I tore off a piece of bread and went into my room, still too full to really eat. I fed a piece to Bibi.

I took my parrot from her cage and let her sit on my shoulder. "Guess what? Summer is here, Bibi! Hiwa and I have big plans for playing video games and lazing around. In July I'll go to my grandmother's village in the mountains. You'll be all right with Dad for a few weeks. I went last year, remember? I made a little calendar for you so you'll see when I'll be back? Hmm?"

Never mind the smell of manure. Never mind the stone walls covered with newspapers to keep out the ceaseless wind. Leyla and Hossein, my cousins, would be there. I would lose myself in the mountains and their beauty and in my daydreams. Summer would be great. But first would come the wedding.

Mohammad and Avin's wedding would last for three days. School was out, and the time came closer and closer. Hiwa and I played soccer in the mornings until it got hot and then hung around Mohammad's house. We decided to put off buying the Pac-Man until after the wedding. That way, we could save a little more money.

At Mohammad's we tried to be helpful, but my mother said we mostly got in the way. This was completely inaccurate! We helped a lot—or I did, while Hiwa sat around making me laugh. I weeded the courtyard, trimmed overhanging branches, and beat the dust out of the carpets. Together Hiwa and I tasted a lot of the walnut pastries and the mixed fruits and candies to see if they were okay.

Two days before the wedding, my grandmother and Leyla came down from Bairan, their village, to help with the last-minute preparations for the groom's side. We would be the hosts for the first night.

"Behar! My daughter! How wonderful this is! And Mohammad!" Nana exclaimed, hugging us one by one. "To see my younger son married! Your brother Kamal was killed in the Iranian Army so young. It's a very special occasion for me to see my son get married, to know Mohammad has survived this long with so many others dead, eh, Azad?"

I squirmed away from Nana. "Leyla! Hi!"

"Hey, Azad!" She grabbed both my hands, and we spun in a circle. "I haven't been in Sardasht in ages. Let's go out. Nana, can we? Before I get stuck doing a thousand chores?"

"Yes, yes." Nana gave us each some coins. "Go on. Have fun."

"Come on, Azad!" Leyla dashed outside. She was dressed in a turquoise tunic and loose pants.

"Wait!" my mother said. "You can't go to the store dressed that way! You have to cover yourself. You know that." She came out with Leyla's black robe and scarf and helped her dress, tucking Leyla's dark brown curls tightly under the scarf. Leyla's brown eyes flashed impishly at me, as if to say, "We'll never get out of here!"

Together we hurried down Gurda Sur, Leyla literally dancing by my side.

"Phew! This is great! It's so good to get out of the village. I really do need to buy a few things."

"Like what?"

"A hairbrush and some barrettes. A mirror in a case so it won't break. And some hand lotion for my mother."

I gave her my coins. "Take this so you'll have enough. And maybe you can get something for Hossein, too."

She stopped. "Hossein? He's such an idiot. All he cares about is joining the resistance, the pesh merga. So what do you suggest I get him? A rifle?"

"Leyla!" I glanced around quickly. She spoke so openly!

"What? I might join, too, when I'm older. Nothing is more important that fighting for Kurdistan. Don't you believe me, Azad? I will!"

"I do. I believe you. But don't talk about this here. Okay?"

We passed the bakery and then my house. After we turned the corner onto the shopping street, I relaxed. Leyla hurried into a ladies' shop while I wandered into a stationery and toy store next door. I looked at the brightly colored yo-yos, coloring books, and pencil sets. Last year we would both have been in here trying to decide which toy to buy. Now Leyla was concerned about her appearance. She didn't need to be. She looked great, much more beautiful than the girls in my neighborhood or Hiwa's sisters.

I went outside to wait. She was taking forever. What on earth was keeping her? Finally she came out, clutching a plastic bag. She leaped and twirled and took my arm. I had to smile. Even though I made fun of Hiwa's poem, I thought of sparkly water when I saw Leyla, water that rushed and played and danced over stones. Was *I* falling in love?

"Guess what I got? Lipstick! See? It's called Deep Plum Rose." She pulled it out of the bag. "For the wedding!"

"Put that back! Keep it in the bag! Are you crazy? Let's go home."

"Okay. Are you sure you don't want anything, Azad? I have some money left."

"No, thanks. So tell me. How come just you and Nana came? Isn't your family coming?"

"My parents and Hossein will come tomorrow evening. I help Nana with everything now. Azad, I want to warn you: Hossein's really changed since last summer. And you have, too! You're so tall. And so quiet."

"Yeah, well . . ."

As we walked slowly up the hill, I pretended that we were a married couple, walking home from a fancy restaurant.

• • •

The day before the feast, Leyla and I set about cleaning up Mohammad's courtyard in earnest. She tucked up her baggy pants, climbed into the pool, and began to pull out black, rotting leaves from the bottom. I had gotten the strings of lights from the bakery. Hiwa arrived with his father's lights while I was dragging a ladder over from the neighbor's.

Together we set up the stepladder and locked the brace in place. "Aren't you going to introduce me to your cousin?" he whispered.

"You don't know Leyla?"

"I have not been properly introduced. Come on, Azad. She's gorgeous! Give me an excuse to talk to her."

How dare he have an instant crush on Leyla when I'd known her my whole life and was just deciding I might have a crush on her! "What about Avin, whose hair is like the mountain torrents? Aren't you madly in love with her? What happened to that?"

"Don't be a jerk! She's way too old for me."

"Yeah. And way too smart."

He glared.

Leyla climbed out of the pool. Her wavy dark hair was parted in the middle and gathered into one thick braid that fell down her back. Droplets of water on her legs sparkled in the sunshine as she dried herself with a towel, smiling at us. "Hi," she said.

"This is my friend Hiwa. Hiwa, Leyla," I said grudgingly. We'd grown up playing together, along with her brother, Hossein, every summer. Now here was Hiwa strutting around her like a peacock.

"Leyla's such a pretty name. Are you raking?" he asked. "Let me help you!" He took the rake from her.

"Okay, thanks." She picked up a short broom to sweep the steps.

"Hiwa? Excuse me? *You* are doing work?" I asked, struggling to wrap the light cord around a wobbly branch. "I hope I don't fall flat on my face from shock."

Hiwa glared at me and mouthed, "Shut up." Vigorously he raked the whole courtyard, every tiny corner, while I strung the lights from the trees and along the garden wall.

"You know, Leyla," Hiwa said, "I might be coming to Bairan to visit Azad for a few days in July."

"You mean your dad's making you go?" I asked.

"My dad said I could. I *want* to go," he said.

"I hope you do come. It'll be fun," Leyla said.

I snorted.

I finished with the lights and knelt beside Leyla to help her sweep the litter from the yard into a plastic bag. "Just ignore him," I muttered.

"Why? He's cute," she said teasingly.

"Leyla!" my grandmother called. "I need you to chop some walnuts for me. I have to rest my back for a minute."

Leyla glanced at me. "Can you finish this?"

"Yeah. Sure."

She ran inside.

Hiwa dropped the rake. It clattered to the ground. "Azad, you creep! What were you doing? Can't you see I like her? Oh!

I know what the problem is. You're jealous. You have a crush on her and you've been keeping it a secret. Right?"

He tickled me on the stomach and I started running. I hated being tickled. "Azad loves Leyla, Azad loves Leyla," he chanted, chasing me.

"No, I don't. I don't love anybody. I think love is dumb."

"Yeah, right. Grow up, Azad." Jokingly, he puffed out his chest. "Be a man!" He raised his arms into body-building postures and flexed his muscles like Mr. Universe.

"Cute. Are you really coming to Bairan?"

"Yeah. My dad said I have to," he answered glumly. "For a day or two."

"That's great! We're going to have so much fun."

"Really? Fun by candlelight? Fun in the outhouse? What kind of fun do you mean? Hey, isn't this yard clean enough? The guests are coming in the dark. They won't notice a few twigs here and there. Let's go to my house for a while."

I picked up the rake and put the ladder away and followed Hiwa out into the street.

His mother and sisters had gone to her village for the day and left us pilaf and beans, which we devoured. Hiwa had gotten an electronics magazine. He dragged me up to his room to show me the pictures of futuristic gadgets he'd been reading about. Robots. Tiny fold-up telephones that you could carry in your pocket. Satellite television. A few people in

Sardasht had satellite dishes, but the magazine said that soon everyone in other countries would have such things. And besides Atari, we could now get stuff from a company called Nintendo.

At least he'd forgotten about Leyla. I had never realized before that I had such strong feelings about her. Did I truly have a crush on her? No, probably not. I loved her because we were old friends. I just didn't want Hiwa barging in on a friendship that was so important to me. Did he think he could just flirt and show off for any pretty girl that walked down the street? I gritted my teeth. It seemed everyone got on my nerves lately in one way or another!

I soon got bored with the magazine. "Let's go down to the field at school. I bet some guys are there."

So we went to the playing field for a while and then hung around the newsstands. Then we went back to Hiwa's and played chess, and I lost.

Around four, I went home. I walked up the hill to my house, thinking about Leyla. She was so spunky and tough, with a certainty and confidence that I knew I lacked. She didn't waste her time lost in doubts and daydreams. We were so different. She knew right away what to do; I could never decide on anything.

My dad was home, sitting on the front steps, smoking.

"Ready to eat?" he asked.

"Sure." I went inside. He'd left two lamb kebabs and a cucumber with sliced tomato for me on the table. He poured himself some tea and sat with me while I ate.

"What have you been up to? You've been playing at Hiwa's this week?" he asked suddenly.

"Yeah. This afternoon I was." I carefully omitted telling him that I'd been helping Uncle Mohammad and Mom get ready for the wedding.

He took a cube of sugar in his teeth and sipped the tea through it. He finished the whole glass of tea this way, then put the cup in the sink. I took my plate to the sink, too.

My father got his jacket from the other room and came back to the kitchen as I started washing the dishes. He stood behind me.

"Azad, remember. I don't want you going to Mohammad's wedding."

I whirled around, my hands, wet and soapy, dripping water onto my pants. "Dad! The wedding's tomorrow! The whole family will be there—Nana, Leyla, Hossein. Hiwa's going, too. I have to go. Why are you trying to stop me?"

"You heard me, Azad. I forbid it."

"Well, I'm going! What's it to you, anyway? You don't care what I do. You don't even know when school is in session or not. All you care about anymore is going out night after night—"

I heard a horn outside, two, three times. Dad did nothing. The horn honked again.

"Who is that?" I asked.

"Just a friend." He crushed his cigarette in the ashtray. "You're getting to be as bad as your mother. Do whatever you want."

And he left.

• • •

The next evening, the bride, her family, and all the guests came to Mohammad's house. To avoid my father, I hung out that afternoon at Hiwa's, and then we walked up the hill together.

"My cousin Hossein should be here," I said excitedly as we entered the courtyard. "There he is!"

Hossein was standing with a group of young men by the doorway of what would be the men's entrance.

"Hey! Hossein! Come on, Hiwa."

"No, I'm going to help Abdullah with the food. I'll be in the garage. Meet me there, all right?"

I ran across the courtyard. "Hossein!"

"Oh. Hi, Azad." He gave me his hand, clasped mine hard, and slapped me on the shoulder. "Cigarette?" he asked, pulling a pack of western Marlboros from his pocket.

"I don't smoke. You know that. What were you guys talking about?"

"Oh, you know . . ." Hossein shrugged. "Nothing much."

The conversation had stopped. There was an awkward silence. They were clearly waiting for me to leave. Then I saw Leyla carrying a tray from the garage to the house, a spangly orange scarf over her hair and the rose-colored lipstick brightening her lips. I crossed the courtyard, glad to get away from Hossein's friends.

"Nice lipstick. You look great!"

"You think so?"

"What's with Hossein? He barely spoke to me."

"He's trying to impress those guys. Don't mind him. He's so full of himself lately. But I have to hurry, Azad. I'm busy."

"Sit next to me inside, okay? Hiwa and I are going to be with the women."

"Sit? You think I'll have time to sit?" She hurried off.

In the neighbor's garage, a barbecue grill was set up in the doorway to cook the kebabs. Small barrel-shaped tin stoves held flat pans of simmering rice, tomatoes with eggplant, lentil stew, and soup. Mohammad and Abdullah, as his best friend, had supervised the cooking, both as nervous as cats. A group of men, including Hiwa and me, formed a line to pass the serving dishes and piles of fresh flatbread into the house, where the guests were seated. We kept peeking out the door to see what was going on.

The women arrived dressed in the brilliant colors of butterflies and spring flowers. So many wildflowers grew on our grassy hillsides—tulips, poppies, narcissus, hyacinths. The long tunics the women wore were red, yellow, pale green, and purple, covered with sparkling colored sequins.

Avin was the most beautiful of all. She wore bright red lipstick, a silver tiara in her hair, a black skirt, and a white blouse with a large, flat lacy collar. Her broad sash was black. Hiwa was beside himself with renewed, unspoken love. I laughed at him. I couldn't help it. Without saying a word, he punched me. Hard.

"Ow! That hurt!" I yelped. I wondered why we were pushing and shoving so much lately. This girl stuff was getting to be a problem. To annoy him, I said, "I think I want to eat with the men."

"No! We should stay with the women and children so I can stare at Avin."

"Give it up, Hiwa! Everyone can see you're in love with her," I said loudly, still irritated because he'd hit me. I passed the last platter of steaming rice to him.

"Would you shut up!" Completely flustered, Hiwa dropped the heavy pan on the floor. Rice flew everywhere!

"What's this? Go, go, you two! Get out of here!" Abdullah rushed at us, shooing us outside like chickens. "Here! I'll even give you money to get you out of the way!"

The other men laughed as, gleefully, Hiwa seized the crumpled bills Abdullah thrust into his hand.

"Look at this, Azad!" he crowed. "Finally! We have enough money for sure to buy the Pac-Man game."

"Yeah. Great. And look how we earned it."

We went into the garden, our argument forgotten. We couldn't stop laughing, thinking of the sticky rice flying into the air. What a mess we'd made. We crossed the courtyard strung with lights, and I started to enter the men's room, but Hiwa tugged my arm.

"Please?" he asked. "It's more fun to listen to the women. They're not so deadly boring. Besides, Leyla will be there. And there might be other cute girls. It's probably the last year we can get away with something like this."

"Okay," I said. "Yeah. If we sit with the men, I'll have to kiss each man four times. All those whiskery faces. Yuck!"

"Don't actually kiss. I don't. I just press my cheek on the side really quick to get it over with."

Inside, the women and children were seated cross-legged on the floor, close together. Kurdish music was playing loudly on the tape deck, and platters of food were spread out in the center of the circle so all could help themselves. My mother and grandmother sat on either side of Avin, and her mother and two sisters sat beside them. My mother patted a place on the floor and squeezed over for me and Hiwa.

My mom was so excited that she hugged me, and I hugged her back. The room seemed charged with a kind of electricity or magic candlelight, making everyone glow, their faces fully alive amid the generous hospitality, dish after dish carefully prepared to honor the guests, as if to say, "This, this is Kurdistan, here in this celebration of marriage, here in the welcoming of our guests." Anyone who came through the door would be instantly enveloped in this warm blanket.

I looked around for some rose jelly and figs. Hiwa had already spotted them and was stuffing his face.

Everyone was chattering in Kurdish. The women were laughing, making jokes, and talking loudly about the duties of a wife and how tiresome men were and how women have to work so hard while all men do is go away to war or to work in Europe, leaving everything to the women. I was a little embarrassed. I realized I was too old to listen idly to this stuff, especially the part about the wifely duties, and that at the next wedding I went to, I would have to sit with the men, whiskery faces or not.

"I think Avin looks tired," Hiwa whispered to me. "Look how pale she is. She's so delicate."

"I hope she's not tired. We'll be dancing until late. Tomorrow we have to do this again at her house. And the third day we have to have the mullah come for the ceremony." Mullahs decided the laws in Iran; they were the censors, and they performed civil ceremonies.

"Remind me to skip that mullah business," Hiwa said.

"Mmmm. This lamb stew is great." He helped himself to another mound of rice, flatbread, and stew.

"Yeah. I made it."

"You did not."

"No, Mohammad did. He's a great cook. Why do you think Avin is marrying him?"

"She's a student, huh?" Hiwa asked, his mouth full. "In what subject?"

"Medicine. She wants to be a doctor."

"Not possible. How many Kurdish women doctors does the government allow?"

"I don't know. A few, I think. As long as they aren't in charge of anything. I might be a doctor, too."

"You? You're going to be a poet. The Flamingo said so."

We burst out laughing. No Kurd would want to be an expert in Persian literature, even though we shared many of the same ancient stories.

Leyla dropped down beside us with a full plate of food and started to eat.

"Seriously, though. When I grow up, I'm going to run a computer store," Hiwa said.

"Come off it. Where will you get computers?" I asked. "Iranian companies will never get around to making stuff like that. They can barely manage to create electricity! You'll have to move to Japan!"

"No I won't. I'll have the computers smuggled in from Turkey. They're not that big. One mule could probably carry four or five. What about you, Leyla?"

"Me? I'm going to be a teacher. In a village school."

I was concerned. "And stay in Bairan forever?"

Leyla shrugged. "Yeah. I love it there. I love the mountains. That's my home."

I had daydreamed of us living in Paris or someplace cosmopolitan and fancy. How was this going to work?

Mohammad arrived, wearing a loose gray jacket with a big sash and loose pants that were tight at the ankles. He sat proudly beside Avin while the photographer took a lot of pictures. Then, when the dishes had been cleared away, the women started dancing in a long line.

Hiwa and I were hot and bored by this time. Unable to eat any more sweets, we went outside and clambered up onto the six-foot-high cinder-block wall that ran around the edge of the courtyard, and sat, swinging our legs from side to side.

"You want to go buy Pac-Man tomorrow?" Hiwa asked, pulling the money out of his pocket and staring at it. "Let's."

"I can't. I have too much to do. Let's go after the wedding. Sunday is best for me. Tomorrow Mohammad and I have to go talk to the mullah and negotiate his fee for the ceremony."

"Don't give him very much. Then he won't talk for hours and hours."

I smiled. Everyone said that—that mullahs tried to talk a lot during the ceremony so they would be paid more. People said that mullahs were corrupt. I didn't know if Mohammad had found a nice one or not. I glanced down the street.

Even though it was dark, at least nine o'clock, I noticed a car parked in the shadows. I stared in disbelief. It was my father's car, the beat-up little black Lada that the secret police had given him. I could see the glow of his cigarette inside.

Suddenly I knew: he wasn't here by accident. He was spying on his own family! He was watching me!

"My dad's here," I said, pointing.

"Really? Why?" Hiwa asked. "Was he invited? I didn't see him inside."

"He wasn't invited," I said shortly. I didn't know what to say. If I told Hiwa my dad was an informer, I might lose him as my best friend because he would be afraid of associating with me. He might turn against me. He'd tell his parents. And what if he told the other kids at school? They would torment me.

I knew Hiwa could sense the abrupt change in my mood. We watched the car for a minute. Then Hiwa said, "Come on, Azad. Let's go back in. Forget about him!"

"You go. I'll come in in a second."

"Okay." He jumped down.

I sat on the wall a little longer, staring at the car. I was breathing hard, my anger growing. I knew my dad wasn't here checking up on me as a nervous, watchful parent. He was here because of his job as a spy. And now I knew the real reason he hadn't wanted me to come tonight—because he had been assigned to watch the wedding.

Boiling up now as if from out of nowhere came the years of rage at being put down, pushed aside, spied on, controlled in every facet of our lives by our absolute ruler, the Ayatollah. My father had accepted his role in this year after year, splitting our family apart, but I'd never thought that he might spy on me. How innocent I'd been to think I was being spared what practically everyone else in my city was subjected to, this constant betrayal.

In a fury, I dashed down the street and banged on the car window, yelling for my father to unlock the door. "Open up! Open up!" I hoped there wasn't a Guard patrol nearby.

My father unlocked the door. I slipped into the passenger seat. I could tell he'd been drinking. Alcohol fumes and cigarette smoke filled the car.

"What are you doing here? I can't believe this! You came to spy on Mohammad and Mom? And me? Are you crazy?" I was screaming. The inside of the car smelled terrible. "And you're drunk. Are they paying you with liquor instead of money? Liquor is illegal, but not for you? You know what? I don't want anything more to do with you. I'm running away. I'm thirteen, old enough to quit school. I don't care where I live. It won't be with you!"

I stopped speaking, spent. I was still breathing hard, but I didn't regret a word. And if he tried to get me to take it back, I wouldn't. I *would* leave. I didn't care where I went.

He didn't answer. He looked down at his hands. He couldn't look me in the eye.

He said in a near whisper, "Mohammad has friends who are Kurd activists. PDKI. And Abdullah was once in the Iranian Army. He knows a lot. He's been trained in military tactics. So he has to be watched. I didn't want them to send someone else, so I said I'd do it. I tried to warn you not to come."

He'd tried to warn me? He should have told me what was going on!

"Azad, don't run away from home. Iran is very dangerous, not just because of the war. There's no need to run away. You can go live with your mother if you want," my father said. "Please try to understand my situation. I must cooperate with my superiors or I'll be imprisoned—or even killed. You're right. You shouldn't stay with me any longer. I'll tell the officials I'm having mental problems and that you had to go stay with your mother for a while."

"Really?" I was stunned. "You'd do that?"

He nodded. "I'll sign the papers this week. You can move after that. But I don't want you running off. Who knows what would happen to you."

He'd said I could go to my mother!

Ever since I was seven, I'd imagined that to be reunited with my mother would be a dream come true. A return to the memory of fountains and rose gardens and home-baked bread and a cozy, sunny safety.

Two weeks ago, before the captain came, I would have been ecstatic. To be away from my father, and finally able to live with my mother in honor and dignity? I looked at my dad. He had his head down and was rubbing the back of his neck.

"Thank you," I said. I felt bad then, ungrateful, as though I'd hurt his feelings. "Dad? What about you?"

"Never mind me," he said. "Go back to the wedding."

I slipped out of the car and ran back toward the house. I wanted to feel happy. But now I knew that Mohammad and his friends were under surveillance, so if I did choose to live there, I would be watched, too.

I leaned against the wall in turmoil, dizzy from the cigarette smoke, the noisy wedding, the crowds of guests, the horrible fumes in the car, the shock of seeing my father defeated and drunk.

Hiwa was inside dancing. I went and sat in the garage with the soiled pots and pans.

"Azad?" Leyla poked her head into the garage. "I was talking with Hiwa. What's going on? Why are you out here?" She sat beside me on the cement floor.

I had to tell someone what happened. "I had a fight with my dad. He's here. Now. Outside, spying on us, Leyla."

"He is? And you yelled at him?"

"Yeah. I'm not going to stay with him anymore."

"Wow. He's going to let you live with Behar?"

"Yeah." I smiled. "Everyone's dancing. You should go back inside."

"No. It's nice and cool here. I missed you inside. That Hiwa is such a show-off."

She laughed, and I felt the knot in my heart ease just a little.

7

By ten the next morning Mohammad and I were walking down Gurda Sur to the mullah's house to discuss the wedding ceremony. I was trying to think of a way to tell my uncle at least some of what had happened last night without spoiling the happiness of his wedding.

"How did you know that you wanted to choose Avin as your bride?" I asked, to start a conversation.

He smiled. "I love her. It was simple."

That didn't seem like a good answer to me. Look at Hiwa—in love with Avin one day, with Leyla the next. The poet Attar said earthly love was something that could easily be lost. Didn't Mohammad know this? "I don't know why anyone bothers with love. It doesn't seem worth it. People can be so rotten," I said.

"Come on, Azad. It's important to trust others."

My mother had been wrong to trust my father. People could change. There had to be more to a lasting love than trust.

We were heading downhill toward the more crowded section of Sardasht. We passed the spring, the reservoir where our fresh water came from.

"Of course," Mohammad continued, "love has to go hand in hand with some other things. Devotion. You have to honor your wife."

Did Hiwa honor Avin? I didn't think so. He hadn't even known she was a medical student. What about my parents? Clearly not!

"You have to be generous in the face of your own needs," Mohammad said.

Why did he always have to speak like a philosopher? Honor. Devotion. Enough about love! I had to tell Mohammad what had happened.

"Last night, Mohammad, my father was assigned to watch the wedding party by the secret police," I said. "I saw him parked outside."

Mohammad tried to smile so I wouldn't feel bad. "That doesn't surprise me," he said, but it came out more bitterly than he'd meant it to.

"It doesn't?"

"No. The regime always watches Kurdish weddings. Their excuse is that we might be planning a revolt any time we get together."

"He was drunk and I yelled at him."

"Look. You must already know this. Omar can't stand up to the police. He does whatever he's told."

"But, Uncle, he has no choice! If he doesn't cooperate he could be killed."

"A man of honor always has a choice."

I frowned. I didn't want to think about that right now.

"Anyway, the good news is he said that I can come live with you if I want to. But I know you're just getting married, Uncle. I don't know if this is—I mean I know it's a bad time to bring this up—but is it okay if I . . ."

"Bad time? Hey! It's not good news. It's great news! Are you crazy, Azad? Of course you can live with us. Don't be silly. You *will* live with us. Just like a son. It's settled. Now, here's the mullah's street." He put his arm over my shoulders as we walked and once or twice pinched my cheek and smiled at me. I hoped he was happy. I felt like an intruder, though, as if I didn't belong anywhere. The timing couldn't have been more awkward.

Two donkey carts stopped in an intersection so the drivers could have a long conversation. They were from different villages and probably hadn't seen each other in months. Everyone patiently edged past without complaint. No one was in that much of a hurry in Sardasht. Where would we go?

While Mohammad negotiated a price with the mullah, I crouched on my haunches beside him, tracing an intricate pattern in the carpet with my finger and thinking. I guess I felt guilty for wanting to leave my dad. He was so pathetic and weak. Would he be all right without me? I wasn't at all sure.

•   •   •

I wanted to talk to my mom as soon as we got home. She, Leyla, and Nana were getting ready to go to Avin's, but I grabbed her by the arm.

"Mom! Come here for a minute!" I pulled her outside. "I have something to tell you."

"Oh, please. What? Has Hiwa gotten into more trouble? Not now, Azad. There's so much to do. We have to go to Avin's and help her mother prepare for tonight. I should be there right now. Can't this wait?" she asked.

"No. It can't. Guess what!" I said, grinning broadly. "Dad says he'll let me come live with you!"

"What? Really? Is it true? Oh, Azad, how wonderful!" She hugged me tightly, crying a little from happiness. "Did he say why? How did this happen?"

I didn't quite know what to say. "We'd been arguing about it for a long time and finally he said okay." That wasn't entirely a lie. "Actually," I added, "I threatened to run away. So he said I could come to you."

"And you told Mohammad, too? Oh, I'm thrilled, Azad. We can help you move as soon as the wedding is over."

"Behar!" Nana called. "We're late."

My mother kissed my cheek and hurried off.

That night, we went to the bride's house for another huge meal and more dancing. Everyone gave gifts to each other. There was more and more and more food. We were clearly tired, trying to paste smiles on our faces and just barely managing. My hand ached from being squeezed in so many handshakes. My cheeks were red where so many older people had pinched them. My bottom was tired from so much sitting. Only the guests seemed as full of energy as ever.

By the third day, I was in a daze. Since Hiwa wasn't there, I sat with the men, kissing their cheeks four times, using Hiwa's cheek-pressing method. After we ate, the mullah performed the wedding ceremony and Mohammad and Avin signed documents committing them to marriage. I wondered if my dad was watching us.

I hugged Leyla and Nana goodbye and went back to my father's house to sleep.

• • •

It was June 28, Pac-Man day at last, but I'd slept late. When I awoke, my father was already at work, so I went next door for my bread and yogurt. I ate while I chatted with Wusta Fatah, then went back home and washed carefully, glad of the peace and quiet. Even though the wedding had ended two days before, I still hadn't recovered. I checked myself in the mirror. It amazed me how fast my hair grew, but still no side-burns, no hint of a mustache. I knelt and prayed, then rolled up the small mat and rushed outside.

Hiwa was ready and waiting for me outside his gate, prov-ing just what I suspected: he was perfectly capable of being prompt if he wanted to be!

"Do you have the money?" I asked, pulling out a handful of coins I'd saved from running errands for Wusta Fatah and from helping with the wedding preparations.

He held up a fistful of crumpled bills. "Let's go."

We started down the hill toward the shopping district, kicking stones.

"You never told me what happened the other night with your father. I forgot to ask. Why was he parked at Moham-mad's?" he asked.

"He was mad that he wasn't invited, I guess," I said lightly. "He was really drunk, too. We got in a huge fight. And I said I was going to run away. Guess what? He said I could go live with my mother."

"Really? And are you going to?" Hiwa asked.

"Yeah. I'm packing my things today. I hate living at my dad's. He's so depressed all the time. There's never any food in the house. I'm tired of scrounging for food at the bakery," I said, hiding my real feelings. "I'm a growing boy. I need a good home-cooked meal once in a while." I knew Hiwa was a big eater and would be distracted if I talked about food. I was right.

"The food at the wedding was fantastic. The baklava. And rice pudding. I love rice pudding."

"You do? It's so blah."

"Exactly. I like blahness."

"I like pastries better."

We passed a small square with a plaque underneath an arched gazebo that commemorated the birth of Zoroaster in Sardasht. He was an Iranian prophet from nearly three thousand years ago who preached that people must choose carefully between good and evil. The name of our city, Sardasht, came from the name Zoroaster. Of course, many cities in western Iran claimed he was born there, too.

"Hey," I said to Hiwa, "Mr. Azizi said that Zoroaster's name meant Golden Camel. And his wife's name was Good Cattle. Remember that?"

"Yeah. Great names. I wonder what kind of kids they had. Half camel, half cow?"

We burst out laughing. "Yeah," I said. "And the Simorgh was part eagle, part dog, part lion, and part bat. That's cute."

"Would you shut up about that ugly Simorgh? Where's Leyla? Is she still around?"

"She went back to Bairan Friday morning. You know, I really don't get this. How can you be so devoted to Avin one moment and then get hung up on Leyla the next? I think there's something wrong with you."

"You're just jealous."

"Yeah. I am. So what? Leyla's my friend, not yours. We've known each other forever. Why don't you get your own girlfriend instead of taking other people's? You snake."

He shoved me. "I'm not a snake. Anyway, you love a parrot. How weird is that?"

"Lay off, Hiwa. Grow up." He was really getting on my nerves.

From out of nowhere, we heard planes above us.

Deafening. Ripping the sky with their noise.

Low-flying and diving lower. Already Hiwa and I cowered and started to turn, pressed back against the wall.

Two of them. They were so close, I could see the metal fuselages above me in detail. How could they fly so low? Were they going to crash? Now I saw two gray bombs falling. Merciful Allah, I thought. I am going to die here by the square. Please, no!

I remembered that moment, caught in my mind like a photograph. Bombs were falling over downtown while we watched, the planes wheeling away like tilting birds, tipping up into the sky, pulled higher and higher by an invisible puppeteer, afraid of what he'd done.

At the same time, I was moving. "Run!" I screamed at Hiwa. "Uphill, quick!" We turned, scrambling, pulling at each other in our haste. We ran close to the wall.

In the next second, the bombs burst, not on the ground, but a hundred feet in the air. And a yellowish dust cloud spread out above the city streets below us.

"Azad!" Hiwa yelled. "Chemicals. Gas. It's the poison. Look!"

"No. Cover your face!" I pulled my shirt up high so that my whole face was covered. I could barely see through the cloth.

Already we could hear people screaming. Already we saw men running madly, some from their houses, from the shops out into the street, from the street into the houses. No one had cloth over his face. Didn't anyone know that was what you were supposed to do?

I tripped and fell against Hiwa. He fell against the wall. My legs were shaking like jelly. He pulled me up. We ran on.

One man ran past us down the hill yelling "Atropine! Atropine." Did he think that was the antidote to poison gas?

A woman swept her child into her coat, covering his face, and shouted "Mustard gas!"

A man running past us shoved me in the chest. "Go home!" he screamed.

We were running, couldn't he see that? My nose now burned horribly. Tears spurted from my eyes. I choked. I smelled something awful. A smell or a taste? It was a taste now. Like bad apples. Or apples mixed with the disinfectant that they used to wash the smelly bathroom at school. My eyes were burning. The cloth of the shirt wasn't enough to protect them. I continued trying to run, blindly. I kept the front of my shirt over my mouth and nose. Hard to see. Hard to breathe. And now I felt nauseous. I struggled not to throw up so we could keep going.

"I can't run," Hiwa said, staggering heavily. I thought he would fall, but I couldn't grab his arm. "Maybe we should walk and not breathe so hard. My lungs, Azad," he gasped.

I turned around to take a peek. The gas cloud sat like a

thick mist in the lowest part of the city. The worst of it had missed us. But even so, the burning sensations kept steadily increasing.

"We have to get indoors. Keep going uphill. Come on!"

We stumbled up the street, running into stalls of fruit set out on the sidewalk, bumping against stopped cars. I lowered my arm, trying to see. Everywhere behind us we could hear screaming. And now we heard the wail of sirens. The air raid alert had come way too late.

"We'll never make it home," Hiwa said, coughing.

The smell seemed much stronger now. The piece of shirt over my mouth didn't keep out the horrible burning taste. I gagged and spat and spat into my sleeve. My stomach heaved. Suddenly I vomited in the street.

We stumbled onto a narrow lane where a school friend, Rostem Salimaniya, lived, and banged on the door, shouting over and over again to be let in. Inside, a dog was barking crazily. How would they ever hear us?

His mother opened the metal courtyard door, her face and hair covered with a towel, and pulled us indoors. She yelled for Rostem's sisters to bring water, and right away she called my uncle and Hiwa's parents.

• • •

Two hours later, Mohammad and his neighbor, their faces wrapped in bath towels, managed to come by car for me and

Hiwa. We had put on layers of the Salimaniyas' heavy clothes, and wet cloths covered our still-burning eyes for the ride up the hill. We kept the car windows rolled up tightly. The streets that had been in chaos for the first ten minutes after the bombs fell were now deserted, as completely silent as they might be during a heavy snowstorm.

We drove to Hiwa's in a state of complete shock as the horror of what had happened finally sank in. Saddam had bombed us with poison gas. We, all of us, every person, our food, our flowers, our air, had been filled with poison. Poison had entered our bodies forever. My body. How would it ever leave again? I had vomited again at Rostem's. Would it help? Was it too late for me? I had breathed the poison, tasted it, felt it burn my eyes and throat. The pain in my lungs kept getting worse and worse.

Babies—I thought of babies. How terrified their mothers must be for them!

We weren't soldiers. We weren't attacking or even threatening anybody. Hiwa and I had been on our way to buy a Pac-Man game, walking downtown. Other people had been shopping or at work. It had been an ordinary June Sunday, but now it was as if the clocks in Sardasht had been smashed at once. No one would be the same after this. Mohammad sat forward in his seat, tensely watching out the window as we drove. He didn't speak. The driver pulled up to Hiwa's courtyard gate and stopped.

Hiwa hugged me goodbye as we dropped him off. Fully covered, his mother opened the gate and waved to us as she rushed him inside.

"We're going to stop at Omar's and get your things. Your father has finished packing for you," Mohammad said shortly.

"What about Bibi?" I asked, barely able to speak.

"Yes, we'll bring Bibi. Of course."

I had promised to protect her, and I hadn't been there. I hugged my aching stomach, sick now with worry about her. How strange my thoughts were. Instead of thinking about war, about leaving my father, about being thrilled to move in with my mother and Mohammad, I was worried about my parrot. As we neared the house, I felt more and more desperate to see if she was all right. I put my hand on the door handle, ready to jump out.

"The air seems okay here. I'll go get Bibi," I said when we pulled up to the house.

"No you won't! You've been exposed to enough of this stuff," Mohammad said. "Stay here and keep that cloth over your mouth and nose. It looks like the dust has settled, but I'm sure we're still breathing in small particles that we can't see. Just listen to me for once, Azad. Sit still!"

I'd never seen Mohammad so tense before. I thought he was going to hit me, and I shrank back in the seat.

The driver tooted the horn for my father to come out. The wait seemed endless. I was crazy with worry.

"My dad won't wrap up Bibi safely when he brings her. I know he won't, Uncle." I grabbed the door handle again. "I'd better go get her."

"Stop it, Azad. Sit still. Didn't you hear me?" Mohammad grabbed my wrist and held it so I couldn't open the door.

My father, his head covered with only a dish towel, came out carrying a large suitcase. To my surprise, in his other hand, wrapped in my blanket, he was holding the birdcage. He'd thought to cover her just in case. Bibi was safe.

He opened my door just enough to put the suitcase inside and hand me Bibi's cage.

"Thank you, Dad," I said, my burned eyes full of tears. I threw my arms around his neck. I heard him draw in a sharp breath, but he said nothing.

He gave me a hard hug. "Thank you, Mohammad, for taking my son."

Mohammad didn't reply. He reached across me and quickly pulled the door closed, telling the driver to start the car and go. I watched out the back window. My father, with the towel on his head and slippers on his feet, stood in the road with a cigarette, watching me drive off, watching me head up Gurda Sur, higher and higher, away from him.

* * *

My mother rushed out to meet the car. She had been waiting, frantic with worry.

"Let me see you. Let me see you." She grabbed my face,
peering into my eyes. "Can you see? Can you breathe? You
were vomiting at Rostem's?"

"Yeah."

"Do you think all the poison left your body?"

"I don't know. I guess so. But I can barely see. Am I going
blind?" I said. My legs had started shaking again. I was shiver-
ing as though bone-cold, but my throat and eyes burned. I felt
limp. Finally the enormity of what had happened hit me fully.
Yet Hiwa and I had escaped. It seemed miraculous. I started to
cry. My mother sat me on the sofa.

Avin rushed to my side. "Listen to me, Azad. You're not going blind," she said calmly. "Your eyes are very sore, but you'll
be fine."

How did she know? I lay back.

My mother draped a blanket over me. "Avin, call the hospital. Ask them what we should do!" she said.

Avin was taking my pulse. She nodded, still counting.

She stood. "His heart rate is fast but steady. Keep him
warm. Rinse his skin with water. Don't lie him flat. Prop him
on some pillows. It'll be easier to breathe that way. I'll try to
call. Draw the curtains, Mohammad."

"Are the planes coming back again?" I asked. My teeth

were chattering now, banging against each other. I wondered if I was in shock.

"No. It's over."

"My stomach hurts."

My mother gently lifted my shirt over my head. Where I'd pulled my shirt up, my stomach had been exposed to the mustard gas, and red blisters were forming patches on my skin. "Look at that!"

"Hush," my mother said, piling several warm blankets on me. She sat beside me with a tub of warm water and carefully sponged off my face, stomach, and arms. My eyes and throat hurt terribly. I wondered if Hiwa was in as much pain as I was.

Avin was unable to get through to the hospital. She made chamomile tea with lemon for me and laid a cool washcloth over my eyes. Mohammad paced back and forth like a caged lion.

"Look at these lesions," my mother whispered.

"It's his throat and eyes that we have to be concerned with," Avin said.

The next two hours were the worst for the pain. But Avin encouraged me every minute.

"Don't worry, Azad. I'm sure your exposure was at a low level. You're doing well. In a week, maybe two, you'll have a complete recovery. You'll see."

"But what about Hiwa? I kept telling him to cover his eyes. Is he okay?"

"I think so, Azad. The important thing is that you and Hiwa weren't in the zone where the bombs were targeted. Now let me take another peek at your throat, okay? Just to make sure there's no swelling. Come on. Open up."

Avin watched me hour by hour. And my mother stayed beside me all night. Avin was right. After three days the pain started to ease up. But daylight hurt my eyes.

Bibi's cage sat on the low table in front of the sofa. I leaned on my elbow and fed her a sunflower seed. She took it, bending her head toward me just as she always did. And at that moment I thought, maybe we will get through this. Maybe somehow things will be okay.

● ● ●

They kept me inside, resting in a darkened room for an entire week, until the pain and swelling in my throat and eyes went down, and the chills and nausea went away. My mom and Avin burned the clothes I had been wearing.

Rostem's mother and Wusta Fatah came to see how I was doing and brought candy and pastries.

Two hundred people had died now, we heard on the news, among them my teacher, Mr. Azizi. And more than four thousand had gone to the hospitals for help with breathing, burns, and vomiting. Considering the whole city had a population of only twelve thousand, that was a terrifying number for us.

And Mr. Azizi, the Gray Flamingo, had already been buried in his village.

The Iranian Army came through looking like spacemen, wearing gas masks and protective suits. They sprayed a heavy white powder on top of the mustard gas dust to deactivate it. One of the bombs had exploded near the city's reservoir, so the water was shut off at first. We had only the water that my mother had stored, and had to make it last.

Mohammad roamed restlessly about the house. During that week Abdullah also came to visit. He knocked at the door and entered, slipping his shoes off.

"Hello, Abdullah. Come in," Avin said.

"How is Azad?"

"Resting."

I waved hello from the sofa.

"But we think he'll be okay. He's tolerating fluids to wash out the poison. His eyes are still a bit burned, so we have the drapes drawn."

Abdullah sat next to me. "You're very lucky. You know that?"

I shrugged. I didn't feel lucky.

"What's this? People have been bringing you chocolates? Oh. Toblerone. From the infidel Swiss!" he teased.

"Yeah." I smiled.

Avin offered him the candy box of chocolate-covered cherries. Abdullah took one.

Mohammad entered and Abdullah stood. They shook hands, immediately going outside to the front steps, where Abdullah lit a cigarette.

Avin said to me, "When the bombs fell, Abdullah went to the center and tried to rescue people, ignoring the danger to himself. He's brave, a hero, but I wish he were more careful."

I watched him talking with Mohammad on the doorstep. Abdullah would bring us real news, not the propaganda we got from Iranian TV.

He and Mohammad talked outside for over an hour. After he left, Mohammad came inside, in a worse mood than ever, walking from window to window. Avin literally tiptoed around the house, preparing the tea from the bottles of stored water. She brought in a tray to serve us, placing it on the low table next to Bibi's cage.

"Please, Mohammad. Have some tea. Tell us what happened," she said. "Is Abdullah all right?"

Mohammad took a glass of tea and stopped pacing.

"Sit," Avin said. "Please."

Finally he sat on the floor beside her. "No, Abdullah is not all right. His brother is in the hospital. His photo shop was hit nearly directly. After the bomb exploded, Abdullah rushed to the shop to help. His brother threw up the gases all over Abdullah and the chemicals in the vomit burned Abdullah's arms. The skin is black under his sleeves. He just showed me. Black! And there was a boy in the shop at the time, a Kurdish boy with one leg who couldn't run away. He's dead. Who knows how many more will die? It wasn't just mustard gas, Abdullah says. Possibly cyanide, to kill people quickly. And there were one or two nerve gases mixed in as well. Sarin and tabun. That's what they think, anyway. The gases make people crazy. They die laughing. It's amazing that Azad and Hiwa are safe."

He bent over and hugged me, then went back to the window and stared out. He walked into the courtyard, but came back in.

"Please, Mohammad, try to relax. You'll just tire yourself. Do you want more tea?" Avin asked.

"I don't know. Yes. Please. So, everyone, here's the news. I must do something. At a time like this, I can't sit around. I've already told Abdullah: I will join the PDKI," he said.

"Mohammad! No!" Avin said.

"Are you sure about this?" my mother asked in a low voice. "You have a family now. Avin's just a bride. You know the risks involved."

"Never mind that," Mohammad said dismissively. "Abdullah's right. The government will make no effort to protect Kurds from Saddam's attacks. His aim is to exterminate us and the Ayatollah won't stop him. Only the Kurdish resistance fighters will help us."

"I think you're making a mistake. Don't be swayed by Abdullah," Avin said. "We've survived so far."

"Barely! Azad was nearly killed! 'We've survived so far.' *We* have, but others haven't. You don't care about those who have died? Are we supposed to sit here and be experimented on like a bunch of rats in a laboratory and do nothing about it? Saddam did this so he can wage his filthy war with the Iranian Army and not have to worry about any Kurds becoming active near the border. What if he kills ten thousand of us next time? Have you thought of that?"

"Please reconsider!" my mother persisted. "People are executed for being in the PDKI."

"People in Iran can be executed for listening to music. For reading books. For wearing lipstick. Of course it's dangerous. But so is sitting here doing nothing. Can't you understand that?"

"Yes," my mother said. "I can. My life became dangerous when I married Omar."

"Omar," Mohammad said with disgust.

"Never mind Omar!" Avin said, her eyes full of tears. "You're the problem this time. You should have discussed this with me, your wife, before making a decision." She stood up and left the room.

The three of us sat in silence.

"She's right," Mohammad said in a low voice. "I should have."

"You've been married less than two weeks," my mother said. "The first months of marriage are hard." She squeezed a tiny slice of lemon into her tea, crushing out every drop.

"Avin!" Mohammad called. "Avin! Come on. Sit beside me here. Please."

Avin came back into the living room and sat down. I could see she'd been crying. "Listen. I was wrong not to discuss it with you. But it's decided, okay?" he said to her gently. "I'll be very careful. Please try not to worry."

"I was so happy before this— What are the real words for this horror?" Tears filled her eyes as she glanced at the drape-covered window. She shook her head. "We were just starting our new life. Who knows where you'll be sent? Into the mountains? Maybe to Iraq?"

"No. I promise I will protect my family first. I won't let this destroy our lives, Avin. Azad is doing better and better. You can all go to the mountains as soon as he's ready to travel. You can relax, get away from this chaos," Mohammad said. "There's that to look forward to."

The stone houses in Bairan were primitive and cold,

and there was endless hard work, especially for the women: herding, cleaning, laundering, preparing dairy food from the goats. But it was the place where Kurds were most free. The mountains could cure us of anything. We'd be safer there.

he day before we went, Mohammad's neighbor drove me and Bibi to my dad's house. I had planned on leaving her with my father, hoping he'd take care of her while I was away. The parrot couldn't survive the high altitude of the Zagros Mountains. The air was thin at nine thousand feet and took a little getting used to. It was no place for parrots; it was a place for eagles and soaring hawks.

"Dad?" I entered the living room. My father was sound asleep in the bedroom, snoring loudly, one arm flung across his forehead. He was clearly hungover. Wow. Sheets, towels, clothes were scattered across the floor.

"Dad?" I said again.

He rolled onto his side, muttering, then opened his eyes and sat up. "Azad! Hi," he mumbled. "Give me a minute."

I went into the kitchen and set Bibi's cage on the table. Dirty dishes were piled in the sink, liquor bottles lay on the table, bread crumbs were strewn everywhere. The place was a mess, much worse than I'd ever seen it.

My dad came to the door, rubbing his face. "Hey, Azad. How are you? What time is it?"

"Nearly four."

"Oh. Things have been kind of crazy here. Sit down. I'll make us some tea. You brought your bird with you?"

"Yes. We're going to Bairan tomorrow." Didn't he remember that he always cared for Bibi while I was away? How could he have forgotten? I quickly changed my plans.

"I'm leaving Bibi at Hiwa's."

"Oh, yeah? Good idea." He stumbled a little, looking for the teapot. Was he safe here by himself? I wondered if I should check on him once in a while. He rinsed two glasses at the sink.

"I'm feeling better now," I said. "From the gas and stuff."

"That's good. That's great."

Was that all he had to say? I sat, feeling the old silence, the years of not talking with him, well up inside me. He didn't seem to notice. He filled the tea urn, scratching his head so that his hair stood up in little tufts while he searched in various little paper bags for some loose tea.

"So. I mean . . . are you okay?" I asked.

"Me? Huh? Yeah. I'm fine." He brought the tea glasses over, sat down, and squinted in the afternoon sunlight and cigarette smoke. Neither of us spoke. "Get that bird off the table," he said.

• • •

After leaving my dad's, I took Bibi, her cage covered, and walked down to Hiwa's. It wasn't far—downhill, a sharp left, another quarter mile—but I soon felt tired and light-headed and my eyes ached. My skin felt as thin as tissue paper, as though it couldn't protect me from anything at all, not even rain.

I knocked on the door.

"Azad!" cried Hiwa's mother. "How are you? You walked here? You must be feeling much stronger."

"I'm fine, I guess. How's Hiwa?"

"Mostly recovered except for his eyes. The doctor said he was only mildly exposed."

Hiwa came thumping down the stairs in his socks. "Look who rose from the dead!" he cried.

"Hiwa! That's not funny! How are you? I came to ask your mom if she could take care of Bibi while I'm in Bairan. We're leaving tomorrow."

"Certainly." Hiwa's mother took the cage. "Bibi, my little one, you're so cute. Would you like a slice of apple? Hmmm? Come on."

"Let's go upstairs," Hiwa said.

We flopped down on his divan. I was exhausted and had to catch my breath.

"You look kind of pale. Do you still feel all weird inside?" Hiwa asked.

"Yeah. It feels like my skin is burning underneath."

"My eyes are the worst thing," he said.

"I told you to cover them."

"You did not. You were as terrified as I was."

"Yeah. Sure I was. Did you hear about Mr. Azizi? He's dead." Tears filled my eyes. The whole scene seemed to sweep back over me like a wave, especially the voices crying out in pain and horror.

"I couldn't believe it when I heard," Hiwa said. "The Gray Flamingo," he said softly.

I cleared my throat and sniffed. After a few moments I said, "So you're definitely coming to Bairan, right?"

He rolled his eyes and pinched his nose shut as if he smelled something bad. "Yeah," he said in a nasal voice. "It seems I have to. I'll come at the end of the month. For two very smelly days."

"Two days! That's it? What good is that?" I took a pillow and whacked him with it. He curled into a ball and let me pound him silly.

• • •

On July 12, my mother, Avin, and I piled ourselves into the Bairan van. Our blankets and suitcases were lashed to the roof, smaller bags wedged in our laps. What should have been a one-hour drive took two hours because of the Guard checkpoints along the road. The soldiers came through the van, pushing down the crowded aisle, demanding I.D.'s, asking questions. The usual boring routine. I just wanted to get to Bairan and this was taking forever.

The van followed the narrow road through its twists and turns and long switchbacks. Twice we had to pull over because I got carsick. When we got off at the bus stop next to the school in Bairan, we were surrounded by village kids. They must have been watching for the van. The driver climbed onto the roof and lowered our things to the ground.

My grandmother and Leyla had walked down from Nana's house, which was at the top of the steep rocky path that wound uphill through the houses. There was no way we could get a ride to her house, so Nana had brought down two donkeys to carry our things. We loaded our blankets, clothes, food—everything—onto the pack frames tied to their bony sides.

Hossein sauntered down from the other side of the village with some guys I'd never seen before, and we shook hands.

"You got your beloved Bibi settled, heh?" Nana asked, handling me candy and pistachios from the pocket of her baggy trousers.

I blushed. I wished she hadn't said that in front of Hossein.

"And how are you feeling now? How are your eyes? Let me look at you. Hmm? You look good as new!"

But I wasn't as good as new. I still felt somewhat scalded inside and out, frail and shaky. I couldn't believe it wasn't noticeable.

My grandmother was a chatterer. She never waited for answers, so I didn't even try. She grabbed ahold of my ears as though they were jug handles. "We'll put you to soak in our fresh mountain stream. You can wash there over and over until all those chemicals are gone."

"Brrr, Nana. That sounds cold." I twisted out of her grasp. I was getting too old to be squeezed and pinched by my grandmother. Besides, Hossein was watching!

"Nonsense. It's wholesome. It's the best thing for you. We'll wash everything of yours in the stream. Your blankets, clothes, everything. And you'll drink only herbal mountain tea that I prepare for you and my yogurt, which you know is the best. My good friend Mostafa has brought you some special orange blossom honey. They say that now Saddam is even killing honeybees in Iraq with those weapons. What a lunatic. He wants to kill everything."

Hossein snorted. "We'll crush Saddam. He'll never take over Kurdistan no matter how much poison he has. See you later, Azad." He headed off up the hill away from the village to join the other men.

Leading the plodding donkeys up the path, we soon reached Nana's house. It was made of flat stones, stacked and held together with daubs of hardened mud. The inside walls were covered with a thick layer of smooth mud and lime wash to keep the wind out. The stone floors were swept clean of loose dirt. The walls were lined with cushions, and the heavy blankets we'd use at night were stacked neatly in the corner of the back room. My poster of Arnold Schwarzenegger, Mr. Universe, was still pasted on the wall. Hossein had given it to me. He worshipped Arnold. But that was last summer.

"Nana, you left my poster up!" I said, smiling.

"Of course I did. Now come on, Azad. Help unload the animals. Their owner wants to take them."

Leyla was bringing in our cooking pans and a large bag of rice we'd brought from Sardasht. Before going out again, she laid some pieces of wood on the cooking fire. Then she went out to bring in the next load.

"Leyla helps me with everything," Nana said. "The pains in my back are so bad."

I saw my mother and Avin exchange glances. Nana had complained about her back at the wedding, come to think of it. Last summer, she'd been so vigorous. She'd climbed to the top of the mountain with me and Hossein several times. She'd ridden on donkeys and carried heavy loads of wood and milked her goats every morning before the sun came up so they could go to pasture.

"Azad, come on! Don't become lazy like Hiwa. Move the bags into the back room and unpack!" my mother said in annoyance. "There's always work to be done in a village. You're not a city boy now."

I hurried outside and lifted our stack of blankets off the donkey, pausing on the stone slab doorstep to look back down at the village. Soft spirals of smoke like spun wool curled from the chimneys. The roofs were made simply of layers of branches piled in crisscross fashion. Everywhere there was the smell of manure from the animals. One of the jobs of the village girls was to clean up the manure, stack it, and dry it for use as fuel in case wood wasn't available.

The houses were scattered down the steep slope in a haphazard zigzag pattern. Nearly on top of one another, they were connected by a series of narrow paths. Chickens rushed everywhere in their frantic search for grain and insects. A few huge, scary, half-wild dogs roamed freely about. They were there for protection against wolves, but because they didn't recognize me the way they did the other kids, they snarled at me, and I was scared to death of them. At the bottom of the hill, where the van had stopped, stood the little stone schoolhouse and the store where the village kids bought juice, chips, batteries, and candy when they could.

The air was fresh and light. Sounds were so different here. In the city, noises jammed together like clouds of dust. Up here, the clack of two stones, the *plock-plock* of donkeys' hooves, kids laughing, each carried separately and clearly on the thin air. I looked around, but Hossein seemed to have disappeared. What was with him, anyway?

I went inside. Only Leyla was there, sweeping out the mud we had just tracked in. Keeping the floor clean was an endless task. Avin, my mother, and my grandmother had already gone to the stream, where a lot of village women would be washing clothes. My grandmother would be eager to show off her son's bride to everyone.

I set the extra blankets in the corner and turned to Leyla. To my surprise, she was crying.

"Leyla! What's wrong?"

She sniffed and wiped her nose. "Promise you won't tell? It's Hossein. Tonight he's leaving with a guy named Zorro. A recruiter for the pesh merga. Those guys he was with, they're from other villages. My parents have been fighting with him about this for months. And then when he heard about the bombs . . . I don't know. Everyone feels like they have to do something now."

"But he's only fifteen!"

"My grandfather said that fourteen is old enough to carry a rifle. Did you know that Saddam is gassing Kurds in Iraq, too? He killed more than two hundred people in a gas attack in April. Iraqi Kurds. The pesh merga say that he wants to kill all of us who live near the border. On both sides. He wants to exterminate us!"

"Who told you that?" I asked.

She shrugged. "Everybody knows."

Extermination of the Kurdish people? Genocide? Why had no one told me? And I had thought Hiwa was an innocent. I knew nothing!

I was mad at my mother. She'd said the chemical attack was an act of genocide, but she hadn't really explained it to me. Why did she always treat me like a child? I was thirteen. My twelve-year-old cousin had to tell me what was going on! Or had I simply refused to understand what the chemical bombs had meant? Hadn't Mohammad said that Saddam was trying to exterminate us? I had dismissed it all because they were upset.

Leyla went on. "I'm sad he's leaving, but—what can you do? It's what he wants. I have to clean up the shed while the goats are up in the pasture," she said. "Are you coming?"

How smoothly Leyla seemed to take things in stride! I trotted after her.

We crossed the narrow path to Nana's stone shed.

"Do you do all the chores at your home, too?" I asked.

"No. My mother does. This spring she sent me to help Nana." Leyla took a short-handled broom and, bending at the

waist, she vigorously swept out the dirty grass bedding, pushing it through the doorway into a pile. Then she took a bucket
of water and sluiced down the floor of the shed, swept it, and
sluiced it again.

"If you don't do this, the goats can get sick," she said, half
to herself. "And the chickens bring in mites in their feathers.
Come on. I have to go get more water for tea and then soak the
lentils." She handed me a bucket, and we set off for the stream.

"How did Hossein enlist?"

"Three days after what happened in Sardasht—July 1
maybe?—a crazy guy named Zorro came through the mountains from Iraq. To recruit boys. My mother was furious about
it, but what could she do?"

"Zorro? He was a Mexican fighter, wasn't he?"

"It's just a code name. Obviously." She smiled at me.
"Probably we shouldn't talk about this anymore. Even the
stones have ears up here, Azad. Be careful what you say, okay?
People are desperate for money. There are jash everywhere.
You can't trust anyone."

We reached the stream. I heard voices farther down-
stream. The women were doing their washing and socializing.

"Don't you want to be with the women now?" I asked
Leyla.

"No. All they talk about is men and babies. Remember
how they chattered at the wedding?"

We scooped up four heavy buckets of water and trudged

back to the house. My dreamy romantic thoughts about Leyla had been abruptly pushed aside, replaced by the demands of village life. My shoulders were aching in minutes, but Leyla never paused to take a rest, and I had too much pride to admit that I couldn't keep up with her.

● ● ●

Nana's house had only two rooms: the front room, which had the shed-like kitchen built off one side of it, and a smaller room in back, where we would spread our mattresses and blankets on the floor at night. The front room was where men visited. And the back room was for women to stay in when there were men visiting. But because my grandfather had died of tuberculosis a few years ago, men seldom came to see my grandmother.

My mother still made me rest every afternoon. Avin set up some pillows and a box under the window. She put her books there so she could study every day, even though school had ended for the summer. I was reading, too. I was determined to read *The Conference of the Birds* this summer in honor of Mr. Azizi.

With Hossein leaving and Leyla busy with chores, I was going to miss Hiwa. I wished I had one of those satellite pocket telephones he was always going on about so I could call him. Instead I'd have to wait for his two-day visit.

That night my mother tucked me in, stroking my hair for a minute. I let her do that once in a while, although I would never have told Hiwa. Having me around was still new for her, after all.

"I wonder if Bibi is okay," I said.

"I'm sure she is."

"When are we going back to Sardasht?" I asked.

"Probably the week before school starts."

"Mom, Leyla told me about Hossein joining the pesh merga and Saddam's plans. Why didn't you explain to me the bomb was part of a plan to exterminate us Kurds?" I said. "You shouldn't keep secrets from me. Leyla's only twelve. She knows everything. No one treats her like a baby."

At first my mother was silent. Then she said, "People grow up faster in the mountains because they have to. That's the reason."

"But still. If you know things like that, you need to tell me. I'm going to be fourteen in October. Maybe because you didn't live with me for six years, you don't realize how old I am."

Instantly I regretted my words. I could see how much I'd hurt her.

"Do you think for one minute that was how I wanted our lives to be?" she asked angrily. "I *had* to leave Omar. For both of us. I acted on principle, Azad, so that you would know right from wrong, even if it meant I couldn't be with you. No matter how hard that was for either one of us to accept, I did it. And I would do it again!"

"But why? Why did you help that little girl?" I was stuck on that one point.

"It wasn't just one little girl, Azad. I joined a secret network of women activists, a human rights network to protect young women and girls. By helping that one girl, I was helping all children. When I was tortured by the police, I told them nothing of my work. They never found the girl," she said proudly.

I was filled with sudden awe for my mother. It was said that no one can withstand the torture methods of SAVAMA. Perhaps they were less harsh in their treatment of women. She had every right to be proud, but I hated to think of her being beaten. I hugged her.

"Good night, Mom." I rolled over on the thin mattress and brushed a few tears from my eyes. I pulled the heavy blanket over my head.

• • •

Roosters were crowing all over the village when someone yanked the cozy blanket from my face.

"Hey!" I said. "Give me that!" I lunged for it.

Leyla looked down at me, laughing quietly. "Ssh," she

whispered, pointing at my mother and Avin, who were still asleep. "Come on. Let's go before I have to start my chores." She dashed outside.

What was she up to? I stumbled after her. The sun wasn't quite up yet, but the sky was aglow. Long bands of orange-pink light played across the snow-covered mountain peaks and the bottoms of the puffy clouds that hung just above our heads. Leyla had brought two donkeys for us to ride. She'd already climbed onto one of them.

"Hurry up, sleepyhead," she said. With the reins, she pulled her donkey's head around and started down the village path at a quick trot, drumming her heels against the donkey's sides. I struggled to catch up, until soon I was jolting along beside her.

We crossed the rushing stream and headed for the bowl-shaped meadow, which had been flower-filled in spring but now was full of dry, mowed grass. Beyond the meadow lay a narrow goat path that led to the mountain peak just behind the village.

"The sun's going to beat us to the top, Azad!" she cried. "Hurry! Let's try to race it!"

She leaned forward, patting her donkey's neck as the animal trudged uphill, and I followed. Halfway up, she slid off. "Never mind the donkeys. They're too slow! They're holding us up." She took hers by the reins and started to run up the goat path, catching herself with her free hand as she slid on the stones.

I jumped off my donkey, completely out of breath now. My heart was pounding from exertion at the high altitude. We ran up the steep slope, stones sliding out from under our feet and clattering down the hill below us. I was gasping for air.

But it was worth it. At the top—dawn, as I had never seen it. The sun rose brilliant, the streaks of pink passing our mountain and hitting the peaks beyond us, touching each, casting it in violet, orange, lavender, the clouds above echoing the colors. Leyla was laughing, spinning in circles. "Look, Azad!" she called. "Look! Kurdistan!"

I stood back at a slight distance, smiling. It was a beautiful scene, glorious, but I knew it wouldn't be my whole life, my fate. Leyla had lived her whole life in one situation. Everything was clear to her. Black and white, good and bad. But I was caught in a fluttery world, a world of insect wings that changed and glinted in the sun. I was struggling to find out just how brave my mother was, and Avin; how complicated Mohammad's decision to join PDKI; how mysterious my brand-new family. And questioning the strange and thrilling choices they made. All this was new to me and I didn't know where it would lead. But now I knew it would never lead me to live in Bairan with Leyla.

Nearly two weeks in the mountains slipped by. I spent my time helping Leyla herd goats, cleaning the shed, fetching water, chopping firewood for the coming winter, and riding donkeys whenever we got the chance. The days were busy, but at night there was nothing to do. There was no electricity. No TV. Only battery-powered radios. And the village store was usually sold out of batteries.

Leyla came over every night, and Nana told stories about the legend of the evil monster who ruled us Kurds in ancient times. He had snakes growing out of his head and ate the brains of children, until he was finally defeated by the valiant blacksmith. And then there was the story about Mem and Zin, the lovers who died together, the Kurdish version of Romeo and Juliet. And there was one about Noah, a Kurd, who saved his flock from the great flood along the Tigris River. The ark had landed not far away—Mount Çurdi in northern Iraq, not Mount Ararat, as the Turks and Armenians said.

As we sat studying in the afternoons, either in the house or by the stream, I noticed that Avin was growing quieter. She seemed pale and had dark circles under her eyes. She barely ate a thing. I wondered if she was sick. Sometimes the mountain elevation made people feel nauseous. Or maybe she missed her family.

We hadn't heard a word from Mohammad in the whole two weeks, even though villagers went into Sardasht every day for one reason or another. Leyla said her family hadn't heard from Hossein since he left, either. I tried not to be particularly worried about Mohammad. He'd promised that PDKI wouldn't cause problems for us. I wanted to believe him.

When I went to my quiet spot at the stream, I often found Avin there, resting in the shade, half-asleep.

"Are you okay? Why don't you go to the laundry place anymore?" I asked.

"I'm tired of hearing them make fun of me, how my husband marries me, a medical student, and then brings me up into the mountains to do back-breaking labor and leaves me."

"That's what they say?"

"Yes. They're terrible gossips. And now they've noticed how tired I am, so . . ."

I didn't get it. "So, what?"

"I think I might be pregnant, Azad." She smiled at me. "Those women can spot a pregnancy a mile off. They can see I am pale and nauseous."

"Pregnant? A baby already? But—what about your studies? Aren't you going to be a doctor?"

"Well, I was. Before the chemical bombs and PDKI and so on. Now who knows?"

"But you're smart, Avin. You shouldn't give up. I mean, it will be great to have a baby, but we should hire a nanny for it so you can continue to study."

She didn't answer for a minute. Then she said, "The bombs, Azad. It was so terrible. I didn't know my life would be like this. If you'd told me, I wouldn't have believed you."

I knew what she meant. Her life had been turned upside down as abruptly and completely as mine.

"What book are you reading?" she asked.

I had brought *The Conference of the Birds* with me, but I was still rereading the first few pages. I showed it to her.

"Oh, I love that poem," she said. She took the book and read a few lines to herself.

I thought, this is what I want. For older people to treat me as an equal. Avin didn't have to tell me she was pregnant, but she did. Just as though we were the same age.

• • •

"Azad, I feel so sorry for your eyes, that burning and those terrible poisons," said Nana one night, stroking my head.

"I feel okay now. Really. Hiwa and I kept our faces covered. I think it helped."

"It helped that you weren't downtown, like so many other people," my mother said.

"When is Hiwa coming to visit?" Leyla asked. "Isn't it soon?"

"Saturday. The twenty-fifth," I said.

"That's tomorrow!" my mother exclaimed.

"Whenever he comes, he's welcome," Nana said placidly.

Hiwa arrived in the early afternoon. I had thought he'd be laden down with his new electronics magazines, tons of clothes, and a soccer ball. But when he got off the van, I saw he had only one plastic bag with him. Leyla and I had run down the hill to meet him by the store.

"Hiwa! How's the big city? Is the poison cleaned up?" I called, anxious for news.

"Yeah. About three hundred people have died. That's the final number. There's really not much on TV about it. I guess the censors don't want us talking." He had an uneasy expression on his face, so I changed the subject.

I took the heavy bag of food. "What's in here?" I asked. "Oranges. Baklava? Your mom made that for me, I bet. What else?"

"Some pickled vegetables. And cucumbers. My mom thinks you guys can't grow vegetables up here or something. Listen—"

"Where's the rest of your stuff?" I interrupted. "Is this it? No soccer ball? No magazines?"

"Azad, listen. I—I have some news for your family."

"Bad news, you mean?" I stopped walking. My heart froze.

"Kind of."

"You should tell everyone, then. Wait a minute." Leyla didn't hesitate. She was already running off to the stream to get my mother and Avin.

"Is it about Mohammad? He hasn't been to visit us once," I said. "Avin is going crazy with worry."

"Well . . . Mohammad, yes. But. It's Abdullah, actually."

I climbed the hill faster, forgetting that Hiwa hadn't had a chance to adjust to the thin mountain air and wouldn't be able to keep up.

"Azad! Stop!" he called out. I waited impatiently for him to catch up. I could see my mother and Avin entering my grandmother's house. As soon as Hiwa reached me, I strode ahead again. Quickly entering the dark room, I kicked off my shoes and set the food on the rough shelf near the stove. Nana poured Hiwa a small glass of Coke and passed it to him with trembling hands.

When we had gone through the formalities of greeting Hiwa and asking about his family, my mother said, "What is it you have to tell us?"

"You know Wusta Fatah? He came to our house last night. He said to tell you that Abdullah was taken by the police maybe a week ago. No one's seen him since."

Avin clapped her hands over her mouth and moaned.

"Did he say anything about Mohammad?" my mother asked.

"Yeah. He said—well, he said the police came for Mohammad, but that he escaped. Neighbors helped him. He's in hiding."

"Allah is merciful," Nana cried, rocking back and forth. Avin ran into the back room and slammed the door. My mother and Leyla were silent. Thank goodness Mohammad had escaped! But what about Abdullah? Sickened, I wondered if Abdullah had already been shot.

I started to cry. I didn't care if Hiwa saw me or not.

"Sorry, Azad. I can only stay tonight. My mother wants me to go straight home. She wouldn't have let me come at all, but I insisted, and Wusta Fatah said it would be okay. She's worried the police might come up here at some point. My dad said he would try to make some inquiries about your uncle. If you want to come back with me and stay at my house for a while, Azad, you can."

"What? Oh. No, thanks." I barely heard him. We could hear Avin sobbing from the next room.

"Hiwa," my mother said, "thank your mother for letting you come. We appreciate the news. Thank Wusta Fatah for us, too."

Hiwa nodded. "Wusta Fatah told me something else, too, Azad. He said—he said your dad is an informer."

I stared at my socks. My big toe peeked out through a large hole in the right one, the edge of the nail pale as a crescent moonrise. "Yeah. That's the real reason I left him." I felt a wedge between us that neither of us wanted to be there. Hiwa had normal parents who played by the rules and went unnoticed. At least so far.

"So," Hiwa said awkwardly. "My mom said . . . I mean, she's—"

My mother broke in. "Hiwa, if your parents want you to associate less with Azad for the time being, that's perfectly understandable."

I glared at her. No it wasn't! I could feel my life being ripped in half—by the bombs, by the regime, by the long war, by how strong or weak people were. The time I dreamed of being a sun-bright coin seemed long past.

My mother spoke calmly. "Maybe it's just for a short while. Who knows? Maybe in a few months all this turmoil will settle down and we won't have to be so careful."

I knew she didn't mean that. She was simply trying to smooth things over for Hiwa. The ramifications of Abdullah's arrest were terrible. And Mohammad could be caught at any moment.

"Yeah," Hiwa said in a relieved voice. "That's what my parents said."

"This stinks!" I said. "Everything stinks."

"Don't worry, Azad. My mom's just nervous. You can still come over," Hiwa said.

"But it won't be the same," I said.

My mother sighed. "What *is* the same, Azad?" She got to her feet and went to comfort Avin.

I left the hut and ran to the waterfall, Hiwa trailing behind me. Leyla was already there. She hugged me fiercely, as if she knew what was coming next and was preparing for it. But I hadn't thought that far ahead.

• • •

Around four, we sat down to eat.

Avin's eyes were swollen with crying. My mother looked pale and nervous. Leyla passed the bread around and served the bean and lentil stew. Only Hiwa had any appetite.

We ate in near silence.

"I knew something like this would happen!" Nana burst out finally. "I always told Mohammad to stay away from Abdullah. You'll all have to flee Iran for now! My only remaining son is a fugitive. I never liked that Abdullah and his big mouth. I told Mohammad a thousand times not to hang around with him, but did he ever listen to me? Why didn't he listen to his mother?" She moaned and rocked back and forth.

Have to flee Iran? I stared at her. Couldn't Mohammad go into hiding? Wouldn't that be the best thing? It was one thing to move to my mother's, but how could I abandon my father? Leave my best friend? My school? My country?

My mother saw my fear. "Nana, please. Mohammad's a grown man. He chose to join PDKI. It's the situation that's caused our problems, not Abdullah." She put her arm around Avin as if to tell her mother that people needed comforting now, not blame.

But Nana couldn't stop. She pointed a knife at Leyla. "You see why I didn't want Hossein joining the pesh merga? Nothing but craziness comes of fighting! I told your parents to keep him out of it. Soon everyone will leave. Soon this village will be an empty ruin! Only the old people and chickens will remain."

Leyla burst into tears.

"Stop it, Nana!" I yelled. "Leave her alone. It's not her fault. Any of this. If you want to blame someone, blame Mohammad! I do!"

I led Leyla outside and we sat on the front step. "She didn't mean it, Leyla. She's old. She's just upset."

Leyla nodded. "But what *will* happen? She might be right. Will you be forced to leave?"

"No way. Come on. Even if Mohammad goes, I'm staying."

"You could stay in the village. We can easily hide you here if necessary," Leyla said. "Why not?"

Hiwa sat beside us. "You won't have to flee, Azad. You can

stay with me. I'll throw colossal tantrums until my parents give in. We already have three kids. Four is no big deal. That way you could still go to school with the rest of us."

"Thanks," I said. "You guys are the best." I buried my face in my arms. They were trying to comfort me, but their words fluttered around me, light and dry like fall leaves.

That night, I tossed and turned. Far off a dog was barking across the village—*woof. Woof woof woof.* And then again—*woof. Woof woof woof.* The same pattern over and over. I was angry with the dog and imagined pelting it with rocks to make it stop barking. Ugh. I was furious!

But was it really Mohammad I was angry with? Avin had been right to mistrust Abdullah, saying that he took too many risks. Had he persuaded Mohammad to join PDKI? Maybe Mohammad didn't realize what would happen now, to all of us. No, Mohammad knew exactly what he was doing.

Irritably I turned over, trying to get comfortable.

First Mom had split up our family by helping a little girl she didn't even know, and now Mohammad had put his life in danger to speak out for Kurds. Why did they *do* these things?

Then I thought of the chemical bombs—how my eyes had burned, how many people were on oxygen, how Mr. Azizi had died. And how Saddam's plan was to exterminate us.

Of course Mohammad had taken a position! He was a good man, generous in the face of his own needs. I smiled, thinking of how he always said philosophical things about life and love. And finally the dog grew quiet, and I went to sleep.

The next morning, Hiwa got ready to leave just as the sun came up. Leyla and I walked him down the steep rocky path to the bus stop.

"Why don't you come back with me now so we can hang out together? These goats and chickens won't notice you're gone. Trust me."

Should I go? Maybe I could do something to help Mohammad. He could be lying in some shed, weak and in pain. He needed a way to get to Bairan. "I don't know. I'll think about it, okay?"

"Goodbye, Hiwa," Leyla said. "Thank your mother for the food."

The dusty, faded-blue van lumbered up the steep hill. Besides Hiwa, there were three old men waiting at the store, each carrying baskets of fresh eggs to sell in the town. As the van got nearer Sardasht, more people would get on with things to sell. My stomach knotted. I couldn't think straight. I couldn't stand how desperately worried Nana, my mom, and Avin were. If I went to Sardasht, could I find Mohammad?

Hiwa got on. "Bye, Azad. Sure you're not coming?"

"I . . . uhh . . . no. Nah. I can't. Maybe next week." I waved.

The door closed and the van started to pull away. I couldn't stand to see it go. I couldn't leave Uncle Mohammad without family, without help. "Wait! Hiwa, tell the driver to stop!" I yelled. I started running. "I'm coming, too." I thumped on the side of the van. "Open the door!" I yelled.

"Tell my mom I went with Hiwa!" I called to Leyla as I climbed on board.

s we bounced down the mountainside, I thought over my rash behavior. What on earth was I doing? I had no way of even finding Mohammad, let alone bringing him to Bairan. I would need help, but I couldn't ask Hiwa to get involved. My dad was my only hope. Maybe for once his connections would be a good thing.

We rounded a hairpin turn, the van lurching dangerously close to the drop-off.

"What's wrong with you?" Hiwa asked. "You haven't said a word. Are you carsick?"

I shook my head. I couldn't tell Hiwa what I was thinking of doing. It had to be a secret. But before going to my dad, I would talk to Wusta Fatah and get the details straight from him.

Two hours later, we got off the van in the city center.

"Come to my house. We need to eat. And you need to see Bibi. I swear my mother's in love with that bird. She's under some kind of parrot-spell just like you."

I smiled, barely listening. We walked through the streets to Hiwa's and sat down for some cold yogurt and pita. I greeted Bibi, lifting her gently from the cage and talking to her. Hiwa's mom was taking good care of her. The cage was clean and no molted feathers littered the floor. I gave Bibi a carrot stick to play with.

Hiwa brought out his latest magazines. There was a lot he wanted to show me. But I couldn't concentrate. I was too restless, and electronics bored me under the best of circumstances. I wanted to go. I wanted to see my house, my street, my father. I had to talk to Wusta Fatah and Hero. Maybe they could take Mohammad to the village and I could go back to living with my dad. If he helped us find Mohammad, I would forgive him everything.

"Listen, Hiwa. I have to go."

"What? Don't you want to hang out?"

"Not right now. I can't. There's something I have to check on. I'll be back, okay?"

Sullenly Hiwa saw me to the door.

"Bye!" I called, and hurried off.

The last time I was in Sardasht, I was still in shock from the attack. Now I felt as if I were coming back to a place that was familiar but that I had somehow never seen before.

I walked up the street from Hiwa's. The town looked different since the chemical attack. There were lots more soldiers and patrols at every corner. I made a sharp right and hurried up the hill to my house. A car was slowly driving up behind me. Someone got out, but I paid no real attention.

"What the hell are you doing?" a voice hissed in my ear. A man seized my arm, hard, dragging me backward. "Why did you come here? Are you trying to get yourself killed?"

I whirled around in fright. It was Wusta Fatah. "I was looking for you!" I said.

"Get in. Come on, come on." He pushed me hurriedly into the side of his van, on top of the bags of flour, and started to drive.

"Why aren't you safe in the mountains, you crazy fool?" he said. "Didn't you get my message?"

"Yes. But Nana said now we would be forced to leave. Flee the country. I came to find Mohammad. There must be another way. Like maybe he could go into hiding or something and I could stay at my dad's when school starts and kind of keep an eye on things there. Maybe things will return to normal."

"What 'normal'?" Wusta Fatah muttered. He pulled up at the side door of the bakery and yanked on the emergency brake, jerking the van to a halt. He turned to face me. "You're out of your mind. You're one crazy kid. You know that? You always did live in a dream world. Here. Help me unload these bags and put them in the storeroom."

Hero rushed into the alley. "Azad! You're here! For a visit? What a surprise!"

"Never mind that, Hero." Fatah brushed her aside. "And don't baby him. Now, please, let us unload these sacks."

Hero retreated to their small kitchen in the far end of the shop, which was also their house.

After I helped Wusta Fatah stack the fifty-pound bags in piles, he slammed the storeroom door shut and locked it with us inside. "Sit down," he said. There were no chairs, so I sat on a flour sack.

He lit a cigarette and stared at me. "So. You came to see your father and find your uncle?"

I nodded.

"You thought you could work something out with your father maybe? Cut a deal with him because he loves you?"

"Yeah. To rescue Mohammad."

"All right. Let's say we rescue Mohammad. And then what was your plan? You go back home and Omar agrees to stop cooperating with the police?"

"Something like that. I would live with him again if he agreed to leave Mohammad alone."

"No!" he shouted at me. "That's ridiculous! No!"

I flinched. "I guess I hadn't really thought it through."

"Fatah?" Hero called, ratting the doorknob. "What are you doing?"

"Stay out of this!" he yelled back. "You've been babied, Azad, by all these women. No one wants to tell you the truth. Life is real. It's not a daydream where you can switch things around and make them come out right in the end. Do you even realize the danger you're in? What if your dad knew you were here? Eh?"

"But my dad wouldn't—" I stopped.

"Your dad wouldn't what?"

I didn't answer. Wusta Fatah shook his finger in my face. "You know what? In a little while, you and I together, we're going to see what your dad will and won't do. Hero! Bring this boy some dinner."

He unlocked the door and opened it. I stood up, ready to leave the storeroom.

"Oh, no, my little runaway. You've done enough running around for one day. You wait here for now and think over what I said. I'll bring your dinner in to you." And he locked the storeroom door again.

I could hear him and Hero arguing about me out in the hall.

"He needs a father, that's what he needs. Every boy needs that. A strong hand once in a while, to show him what's what. That kid lives in his daydreams. He always has. Leave him to me, Hero. Just stay out of this." Their voices faded as they left the hall and went to their room in the back.

I curled up on a sack and sneezed. A puff of fine white flour rose around my head. I sneezed again. I fell asleep and woke up when the baker brought me a tray of food with tea to drink. He sat companionably on a sack of flour.

"So. Tell me about the village. How's your nana?"

"Pretty good. Her back hurts. She has to have help. Leyla helps her. And let's see. Avin's pregnant. At least, she thinks she might be."

"Oh ho! That didn't take long!"

"The news about Abdullah being captured has been really hard on her. Hiwa came."

"Yes, yes, I know Hiwa came," he said impatiently.

"Well, yeah. And my cousin Hossein went to join the pesh merga. No one's heard from him. I guess that's it. Not much happens in Bairan. Fatah? What is it you're going to show me about my dad?"

"Reality, my friend. The beginning and ending of things. It won't be too long now." He looked at his watch. "Just after sundown. The shadows will reveal all." He grinned and winked at me. "Early tomorrow, at six maybe, when people are awake but not too awake, we'll go and find Mohammad with the van. I agree. He's safer elsewhere."

So Wusta Fatah knew where Mohammad was! He would help me get my uncle to Bairan.

He led me to the front of the shop, carrying two glasses of

tea. The display window and door had bead curtains drawn across them and the lights were off inside the bakery. He pulled two café chairs to the front, by the door, but far enough back so we couldn't be seen from the outside.

I sat down and spooned sugar into my tea.

"Now we wait."

We sat there for nearly an hour as the shadows around us deepened. I counted four large flies buzzing noisily near the ceiling fan and I wanted to climb up to try swatting them, but Fatah wouldn't let me.

I could see a rectangle of light in the street from the window of the house next door, my house. My father was home!

And then a Toyota Land Cruiser jolted up the street, pulling to an abrupt halt in front of my house. The headlights were turned off. Then the light in the window flicked off: the rectangle in the street went dark. Two big guys got out. SAVAMA guys. The worst. And then there was my dad coming out of our gate. One of the men clapped him on the back. My dad laughed and got into the Land Cruiser. They started the engine again and drove off.

"That," said Wusta Fatah, "is reality. Do you see it? Do you understand? Your father is ruled by one thing—fear. And such men are very dangerous."

I buried my head and started to cry. I couldn't ignore my father's choices. I had wanted once to help him, but I couldn't.

I couldn't pretend that he would never hurt me. So now it did come down to honor. Making a generous choice, one that would help my new family. When the time came, I would have to leave Hiwa behind.

Fatah sat patiently watching me. A half hour must have passed.

Finally I said, "If we leave, and if I don't see Hiwa, can you ask him to keep Bibi for me?"

The baker nodded. "Hero has made up a bed for you in the storeroom. It's a bit dusty in there, but nice and quiet. Okay? We're getting up early tomorrow." And then he went out.

● ● ●

I woke to the smell of warm, baking bread. I jumped up and put on my pants and the baker's big slippers, then hurried into the hallway.

"Back here!" a voice called.

I whirled around. It was Mohammad, sitting at Hero's kitchen table in the back of the shop.

"Mohammad!" I stared in amazement. "What happened? Are you—"

"Ssssh!"

I ran into the kitchen and hugged him. Even though I knew he had probably been beaten, I was shocked by what I saw. His arm was bound in a sling, his face was swollen and bruised, and he had a patch over his eye.

"I know. It looks bad. But I'm okay." He hugged me with his good arm.

Wusta Fatah beamed from the doorway.

"You're coming back with me to Bairan, Mohammad, right?" I asked anxiously. "Everyone's so worried."

He smiled. "You think the mountains will cure me?"

I nodded. "We can hide you. You'll be safe."

He laughed. "You sound like Nana!"

During the trip to Bairan, I was scared. Mohammad and I lay on the floor of the van, covered with empty sacks and stacks of bread, wedged between some of the sacks of flour I'd unloaded the day before. When we stopped at the first checkpoint, I lay frozen with fright, but no one seemed particularly interested in a baker delivering bread early in the morning. At the second checkpoint, we were simply waved through.

Avin threw her arms around Mohammad. She hugged him fiercely, rocking him from side to side.

"Hey! Watch it!" he said. "You're mauling me. Don't forget, I have bruises everywhere! Never mind me. How are you?"

"Fine! Fine! Guess what, Mohammad?"

"Guess what?" He was puzzled. Then he looked at her face. "A baby?"

"Yes. I am sure I am pregnant!"

Nana kept grabbing the top of his head and kissing it. "I couldn't bear to lose my second son," she cried out. "But you're all right, Allah be praised."

"Mohammad, please. What happened exactly?" Avin said. "Is your arm broken?"

"No. My elbow was dislocated. The police broke down the door of the house around 3:00 a.m. But I had heard their Toyota drive up outside and was already awake. I'd barely been able to sleep since they'd taken Abdullah the week before. I was up, in the hall. They burst into the house and grabbed my arm. I twisted it—that's when I hurt it—and slipped out of my shirt and jumped out the back window."

"That's a drop of nearly three meters!" Avin said. "You could have broken your ankle."

"I jumped the garden wall and the next one and took off down the narrowest alley I could find. A neighbor let me in, and from there I had help. But it's Abdullah I'm worried about. I'm sure he has been executed. There's no doubt the secret police will find a way to implicate me in a conspiracy to overthrow the regime."

No one spoke. He looked at us.

"It's what to do next that's the problem. I could go into hiding in Iran for the next five or ten years. But that would leave you in danger because they would keep surveillance on you in order to find me. And because of Azad's age, I'm not going to do that. Who knows what they might do to him."

Avin meanwhile had unbuttoned the top buttons of his shirt. Mohammad's chest was wrapped with gauze strips.

"Oh!" she gasped. "Were you shot? Is this a dressing for a wound?"

"No, no." He pulled away and rebuttoned his shirt. "A couple of broken ribs. Listen, please. The bruises don't matter. I'm leaving for Turkey as soon as I've finalized the arrangements.

We're all going. We'll claim political asylum there. We'll register with the UN refugee office in Ankara."

"Turkey? Leave Iran for good? No! We can't!" Avin let out a wail. "What about my mother? My sisters? Where will the baby be born?"

"We have to go, believe me. I have no doubt I will be executed the second time they catch me. PDKI gave me enough money to get you all out with a smuggler. When I get to Turkey and find an apartment, I'll send for you and then you'll cross. It won't be easy, but we have no choice."

"Leyla," my mother said, remembering she was there. "You'd better go home. And please. Not a word. Make any excuses you have to, but don't tell anyone for now."

Leyla nodded, unable to look at us. She slipped out the door and hurried home. Mohammad continued talking, outlining our plans. But I couldn't stand to listen.

Even though it wasn't perfect, Iran was my country. My ancient and beautiful country. And so was mountainous Kurdistan, the land full of flowers and spring meadows, waterfalls, dawn, and cold, star-filled nights. My small family was going to be torn apart in an effort to save ourselves. What a contradiction that was. To be saved and destroyed at the same time. To lose everything to try to gain freedom.

"Don't be afraid, Azad." My mother gathered me close.

How brave she was. Nana, too, for facing a lifetime of loneliness fearlessly. I looked around at them. This was my family now. These brave people.

My mother spoke to me reassuringly. "I'm sure Mohammad can find a reliable smuggler, who'll take us safely. The hard part of the journey will be very short. Six or seven hours by horseback through the high passes. A night at the most. The Turkish border patrol makes a lot of money letting smugglers through. We'll be all right, Azad."

I thought of my dad climbing into the Toyota with the SAVAMA guys, how Abdullah must have died, Hossein going off to fight, what my mother had been through to help Iran's young women. Mohammad had done the right thing by taking action, but we also had to take care of ourselves.

I looked at Avin and tried to smile. In eight months, I would have a little cousin. I wanted the baby to be safe. I got up and hugged Mohammad. "I'm glad you're back," I said. Then I went to the back room, where I rolled myself up in my blanket.

My mother came in and touched my shoulder. "Azad?" she said.

"I'm okay." I pulled my shoulder away and kept my eyes closed, too sad to talk. She sat by me for a moment but I wouldn't turn over, even though I was glad she was there.

Gradually, I fell—slipping, falling, spinning into sleep. I

saw the flashes of falling light—yellow, gray, yellow, gray. Butterfly wings or coins. Sun-bright coins falling into a dark chasm.

• • •

Very early in the morning, while the roosters were crowing, I could hear Mohammad talking with my mother and Avin as he prepared to leave. Mohammad would go by bus to the northern city of Orumiyeh and from there cross the twenty or thirty miles into Turkey. When he sent for us, Avin, my mom, and I would be making the same trip.

We'd be leaving sunlight and entering a world of shadowy loneliness. We'd know no one!

I pushed back my blanket and got up, smoothing down my spiky hair and hurrying outside, where a small crowd had gathered to see Mohammad off. One of my distant uncles had come with a car to take him to the nearest bus station on the highway leading north. The men from the village stepped forward and shook hands with him. The women held their children back at a polite distance.

Avin and my grandmother were busy putting food into his bag: figs, bread, cheese, chocolate. My mother watched silently, her arm wrapped across her stomach as if it ached, her other hand at her mouth. I started to cry. Nana tried to hold me, but I took off, running blindly to the shelter of the trees overhanging the stream. When I cried by the rushing water, no one could hear my sobs.

Leyla came and sat beside me and wiped my tears with the palms of her hands. I leaned against her and we held each other. Soon I, too, would leave Iran, perhaps forever.

Epilogue

Mohammad's plan was a desperate one. We all knew that Turkish soldiers and police persecuted Kurds and refused them political asylum.

The two months that we waited at Nana's house for Mohammad to send for us were a nightmare of anxiety. Had he been caught immediately—tricked by his smuggler for money and turned in to the Turkish police? If so, he'd probably been deported, tortured, and executed, and we would never know for certain.

Avin cried every day, even though my mother urged her to stay calm for the baby's sake. The last week of September, word finally came. We would cross the mountainous border near Orumiyeh, then travel with false documents into eastern Turkey and on to Diyarbakir, where Mohammad would wait for us.

We took a bus to Orumiyeh. After the mountain village we'd been staying in, the city seemed chaotic, dirty, and noisy.

The smuggler met us at the bus station and drove us six hours up mountainous roads and rocky tracks to a tiny village. That night we left by mule.

After an exhausting seven hours' ride through the heavy, wet snow, we crossed a cut barbed-wire fence and entered Turkey. For two days we stayed in a goatherd's hut, waiting for our false documents. Mine had on it a photograph of an eighteen-year-old boy who looked nothing like me. We would be driving through dozens of checkpoints and I was sure I would be caught at the first one and sent back.

Still, as we drove the long hours to Diyarbakir, we were excited, certain that we would soon be registered as political refugees with the office of the United Nations High Commissioner for Refugees, as Mohammad had promised. We would be safe!

Mohammad met us at the bus station. Avin was ecstatic, but I could immediately sense fatigue and worry in Mohammad's eyes. For two months he'd repeatedly gone to the UNHCR office in Ankara, the capital city, and each time his claim for political asylum had been turned down. He had taken all the money we had left and hired a lawyer, but who knew what the outcome would be.

We were still fugitives. All of us. So again we went into hiding, this time in the largest city in Turkey.

Istanbul. There I realized we had left Asia behind—its

mournfulness, its poetry, its fabulous beauty, timeless mountains, and ravines of deep emotions. We'd traded it for a kind of busy, pushy, crowded place I didn't understand, a world of electronics and industry and foreignness. I became an uncle! In March, Avin had a baby girl. She said I could name her, and I named her Leyla because of her round, dark brown eyes that were just like my cousin's.

And finally, after eighteen months, the lawyer was successful and we were allowed to travel to a new country. The UNHCR had decided we would go to America. To Maine, near Canada.

• • •

I took the window seat, of course. My mother had to sit in the middle, next to a stranger. Mohammad, baby Leyla, and Avin were across the aisle. I buckled my seat belt and pulled out the travel magazine, flipping to the world map. The plane's route was a long red line, arcing across Europe and then the Atlantic Ocean. Five thousand miles? How many kilometers?

The engines roared louder and louder as we accelerated. The runway was rough, and the plane wobbled slightly from side to side. I gripped the hand rests of my seat, trying to pull the plane up. Across the aisle, Avin clung to Mohammad's hand, her eyes closed. The front of the plane tilted upwards and a little pinging bell rang. *Ping. Ping.* We tilted left, lifting higher. Istanbul's minarets and domes and tiny houses spread out below. The curve of the harbor. Tankers and bridges looked like toys. We were flying like the birds, like the great Simorgh!

A wisp of cloud flashed by the window. Clouds? I wasn't sure what would happen when we hit them. Were they firm? No. The plane slipped through. As we were surrounded by grayness, light diminished, and suddenly the grayness was gone. The brilliant sun shone on a ground no longer hard, nor green nor brown but white. Strange, towering soft white shapes curved across the vast stretch of the faraway horizon. Another glimmering world, with the struggles of people far down below.

Goodbye, Bibi!

I pressed my forehead against the ice-cold window. I was in a place of new dawns, new dusks, new sunlight shining on things I had never imagined before. I was in the land of the birds, part of the sky itself. In the glass, I saw a little of my own reflection superimposed on the grandeur of the sky.

The plane turned once more and we headed west toward my future, the roses of Sardasht tucked in my heart.